T0160615

"Tara Jepsen's LIKE A DOG is outrageously funny and soul-scrapingly grim, in the tradition of our most intrepid, shameless, and shame-filled comedians and storytellers. It also announces a singular new voice in American fiction—one which is deeply alive, hard-hitting, and tender." — MAGGIE NELSON, author of *The Argonauts*

"This book beat the crap out of me. I am bruised and laughing. Thank you Tara Jepsen, may I have another?" — DANIEL HANDLER, author of *All The Dirty Parts*

"Tara Jepsen captures the absurd, animal humor of residing in a human female body on planet Earth like no other, and *Like a Dog* sets it loose within a hazy California underground of abandoned skate pools, weed farms and comedy open mics. Eccentric and insidery, taking on the bonds of family and addiction, the effort to find a life and the drive to end it, *Like a Dog* brims with hyper-conscious gems of hilarity and pathos." — MICHELLE TEA, author of *Black Wave*

"Jepsen proves herself a master of fusing humor and tragedy as she takes us on a psychological road trip through California's suburban wastelands, its cities of hope, and rural cash crop operations, mixing no less than legal skateboarding adventures, fierce, quirky desire, and tragic loss into a powerful and familiar coming of age story." — BETH STEPHENS, artist and filmmaker

"Tara's stories about sibling love, the struggle of drug addiction, and the bonding power of skateboard culture, will break reader's hearts wide open. So detailed and real, it's like being there. This book captures the gritty, feisty spirit of Sister Spit at its best." — ANNIE SPRINKLE, author of *Hardcore from the Heart*

"Tara Jepsen's blunt eloquence takes us deep into the difficulty of our desires, where the things we most want—intimacy, realness, safety, guarantees—are the things we are the least likely to get. In the desolate hardscapes and nowheres of California, north and south, she reveals how closeness can still be alienating: a brutal fact of her stark realism that brings both laughter and tears." — KAREN TONGSON, author of *Relocations: Queer Suburban Imaginaries*

"How can this be Tara Jepsen's first book? Her inimitable voice has been a beloved part of the underground art scene for years—in comedy, performance, and personal essays. With her fiction debut, she turns all her pathos and humor on her protagonist Paloma as she explores the eternal pursuit for love and meaning among and between humans. Jepsen's specialty is the off-kilter observation or indignant proclamation that hits you in the funny bone and then resonates with real soul. I loved this book. I'm ecstatic she could lasso her eccentric and significant cosmology and weave it into this beautiful story." — BETH LISICK, author of *Yokohama Threeway and Other Stories*

"Tara Jepsen's protagonist is a frenetic pinball in a machine of hilarity, recklessness, and existential ennui. Mining the MTV generation's legacy of self-doubt, substance abuse, and unappeasable search for meaning, Jepsen excavates a queer feminist parable of survival that is simultaneously bombastic and completely peaceful at it's core." — ZACKARY DRUCKER, artist, producer on *Transparent*

Like a Dog

Like a Dog

TARA JEPSEN

CITY LIGHTS SisterSpit

City Lights Books | San Francisco

Copyright © 2017 by Tara Jepsen
All rights reserved

Cover photo by Tara Jepsen

Library of Congress Cataloging-in-Publication Data
Names: Jepsen, Tara, author.
Title: Like a dog / Tara Jepsen.
Description: San Francisco : City Lights Publishers, [2017] | Series: City
    Lights/sister spit
Identifiers: LCCN 2017022443 (print) | LCCN 2017032370 (ebook) |
ISBN
    9780872867352 | ISBN 9780872867345 (softcover)
Subjects: LCSH: Self-actualization (Psychology) in women—Fiction. |
    Self-realization in women—Fiction. | Brothers and sisters—Fiction. |
    Drug addicts—Fiction. | BISAC: FICTION / Literary. | FICTION /
    Contemporary Women. | FICTION / Coming of Age. | FICTION /
Family Life. |
    GSAFD: Humorous fiction.
Classification: LCC PS3610.E675 (ebook) | LCC PS3610.E675 L55 2017
(print) |
    DDC 813/.6—dc23
LC record available at https://lccn.loc.gov/2017022443

City Lights Books are published at the City Lights Bookstore
261 Columbus Avenue, San Francisco, CA 94133
www.citylights.com

For Travis, obviously.

I sit on a dirty, flat rock, wearing a hot pink sports bra and boxer shorts, staring into a small fire. I am an arboreal flower with two idiot pistils, my arms. My brother Peter and I are in Idyllwild camping. The San Bernardino forest is a panoply of pine pleasures, the stuff potpourris are named after. The olfactory environs a certain segment of plug-in air fresheners and cleaning products aim to evoke. You are cleaning, but you are also planting a grove of evergreens.

I can eat anything for breakfast. Canned ravioli, pizza, ice cream, it's all fine with my road-dog iron stomach. Right now, I'm roasting two wieners on a long fork for breakfast and after I eat those, I plan to toast some marshmallows. Main dish, dessert. That's proper meal structure.

I hear the quick whistle of the zipper on my brother's tent. He emerges with his long hair in a wild golden snarl around his head. What a beautiful dude. He pats it down, and draws on his menthol. He picked up that habit in prison, the dummy. My mom is not a fan. She's been teaching smoking cessation classes for thirty years so this is probably an accurate place to say, "That's ironic."

"Hi," I say. I approach Peter like he's a feral cat. Slowly, intuitively. Neither of us likes surprises or changes in course.

We like gentle tones. You might perceive a level of chaos looking at us, owing to the tattoos and well-worn clothing, but we're more like high-strung pacifists. Tense buddhas.

"Good morning, Paloma," he says with mock formality. "Is the coffee stuff still out?" I point him to the Jetboil, which gets water ready in mere moments. There is so much rad innovation in camping gear. I bet if you told REI that curing breast cancer would be a great camping accessory, there would be funding and a cure in an instant.

"You want a hot dog?"

"Not yet. Coffee first." Peter sits on a low chair we brought. He smokes, looking at the sky through some towering pines. A hawk or vulture or something flies over us, a singular tear in the cloudless blue.

We're going to Yucca Valley to skate a pool today, someone's backyard spot that won't be around much longer because the house was bought, and the renters are being kicked out. We drove down from San Francisco to ride it, after a heads-up from a friend down here.

I consider cracking open a beer, just the crappy kind that's mostly water, like a Pabst. A breakfast beer. But I have to consider Peter, who has only been clean and sober for two months. The whole family is hoping that this round sticks. Realistically, he will be around people who drink, so I keep telling him he has to get ready for that. He says it's no problem, but I can tell he's doubtful, or annoyed, or something. Regardless, I decide to wait to have a beer. I can always run out to the car and slam one while he skates. Peter is such a jerk when he's on dope, I want to do everything I can to support his sobriety.

I decide I can't wait and take a walk around the campground. I grab a beer from my stash in the truck and slide it into a spongy coozie. The camping spots around us are about half full (note my optimism). I can tell some people have been here a really long time, probably years. I pass a guy sitting at a picnic table, a long white beard hanging from his pillowy, pink face. He is a large gentleman, his body the shape of an upended boulder. His thick feet are crossed under the table, shod in water sandals. If the psychic vibe around him were a perfume, I would describe it as acrid, stormy, and suicidal. Disenfranchised: the new scent from Calvin Klein. His eyes slowly rise up and I move on quickly, looking away. I try not to lock eyes with the violently discomfited, unless a friend introduces us.

I see a lady hanging laundry on a rope tied between two trees. She wears crisp, pink shorts creased down the front of each leg, and a pastel plaid blouse. She's focused. I'm trying to get my beer down quickly so I can toss the can and get through my burps before returning to Peter. I wave to the lady, but she doesn't look up.

We pull up to an inauspicious ranch-style house in Yucca Valley. There's a Toyota pickup backed into the driveway, and the front door is open. There's a small pink plastic Jeep next to the front door, and a couple other playthings evidencing a child. The Toyota starts out of the driveway, and I jump out to catch them.

"Hey, my friend Kevin gave me your address, is it cool if we skate?"

"Hell yeah, he told me you were coming. He didn't tell me there would be a chick skater, that's rad!"

"Yep. Thank you!" The choice not to say something bitchy in response to "chick skater" makes me feel wild and free, a genius of picking my battles.

We grab our boards and shuffle down the driveway through some dusty desert weeds. Inside, there's a sunken living room with a large drum kit set up, and lots of U-Haul moving boxes. A couple huge, black speakers are clustered near the door with some mic stands. A dude with a red mohawk says hello and we show ourselves out to the backyard, where some concrete steps lead down to a small, empty right-hand kidney. There's a red anarchy symbol graffitied on one side, and a bunch of random other tags. All the vegetation in the yard is dead except for a persistent light blue wallflower straggling out from the fence near us. Peter immediately gets in the pool and rides a backside line over the light, ollies over the hip, then grabs his board and stares at the deep end. He lines up a frontside double-double, then stops and pulls his hair back.

"Get in here!" he yells. So I do. We skate hard for an hour or so, then sit on the side panting, wiping sweat, drinking water. We let our legs dangle into the shallow end, like kids at a birthday party.

"This is the best shit," Peter says.

"It's fucking rad that we get to do this again."

"Yeah, that was stupid. I'm stupid."

"Does it feel crazy to skate sober?" I ask, hoping he won't get mad.

"It's weird. For sure." He pauses. "I'm trying to think, was I always high when I skated? Because it feels like I'm kind of learning again."

"Your version of 'learning' is most people's 'years of work,'" I say.

I try to imagine what he looks like to someone who didn't grow up with him. What he looked like to people in prison. I guess one of the guards called him "Babyface" because he has good skin. He should look like Keith Richards but instead, he looks like a Gerber baby. His eyes look like they've changed shape subtly. When he was using, they were cloudier, harder to read. As I say that, I realize it's pretty pedantic. An easy interpretation. Maybe it's muscular. Maybe different choices or ways of living can affect your face's layout. Something your eye measures instinctively: distances between features, proportion.

"Was there another spot around here?"

"Kevin told me about another one in Landers."

"Let's go."

We arrive in a cul-de-sac, and park down the street from the house. My brother waits in the car and I go to the front door. I knock, and hear someone shuffling around inside. A lady cracks the door open, probably in her fifties. A teenage boy stands behind her, trying to get a look at me.

"Hola," I say. "Hay una piscina vacía aquí?"

"Sí," she says.

"Nos permitiría patinarla?" I ask. My Spanish is rough, but close enough. This pool has been going for years, so I know it's an easy get. I take out twenty dollars and hand it to her.

"Sí, pase, pase," she says. I signal to my brother, and she closes the door. We go to the gate at the side of the house. The wood is jagged and weather-worn. I pull on the handle and the gate scrapes heavily across the pavement. I open it just far enough to enter, and my brother follows, closing the gate behind him. We walk down an alley strewn with broken toys, random sun-bleached kitchen appliances, and weeds. We find an egg-shaped pool. It's white with two rows of square, cerulean blue tile at the top. Just past the pool, the ocean of garbage continues. Broken bicycles, garbage cans, broken grills, a stroller, a couple vacuum cleaners, some faded cardboard boxes, a wheelchair, and much more abandoned miscellany. I walk around the perimeter of the empty pool and look down the sides at the transition, which is fairly generous. Peter tries out a scum line. I feel in more harmony with him than I have in years. When he's using, he's so awful to be around.

I don't know when exactly Peter started messing around with drugs, and I doubt I would have found it notable at the time. I did all the teenage lite recreational ding-dongery a person can do: smoking weed, the occasional acid, blackout drinking. I don't think it was abnormal for our age. I remember finding Peter on the floor in our upstairs bathroom one time, shivering. He had on red soccer shorts and no shirt. He looked like your average teen novel character who would have dated a popular girl. I asked him what was going on and he said to call an ambulance, so I did. I remember feeling very scared. It's one of the only memories I have of not paving over my feelings and staying removed from him. It feels raw and embarrassing to think of caring about him so openly. Like that kind of feeling would isolate me, because who would join me on my soft island or even acknowledge that it's on the map? No one in my home.

I didn't find out what the EMTs said about Peter that time. Maybe they just said he was dehydrated? I don't think it was too long after that that he went camping with my parents and I stayed behind in the house. I was supposed to go with them but he was always more of a team player than me and I felt grossed out by whatever trashy car camping we would do, and the false gestures of familial connection. I woke up in the middle of the night and heard a chair scrape in the kitch-en, and then some kind of movement down the hallway in Peter's bedroom. I was terrified. But I also had to pee. Which

I would think would have been overruled by fear. But my ability to compartmentalize was at dissociative, mafia levels. So I walked to the bathroom. The noises stopped. I peed. I went back to bed and willed myself back to sleep with all of my powers of denial. A crushing fist to the heightened animal response within me.

The next morning, I remember feeling uncertain if anything had happened, or if I had dreamt it. This was my go-to mental state for any experience. A self-imposed, cloudy stoner policy that was easier than truth and clarity. I looked around and couldn't find anything that stood out, until I found the broken handle of the back door. When Peter got home with my parents on Sunday night I told them, and Peter ran to his room. They had stolen his video game console, some cash he had lying around, and anything else they could find with a modicum of value. They did not touch the rest of the house. I asked him who the people were and he just said they were dudes in a motorcycle club. He didn't tell me why they broke in, or how they knew what room to target, but later, I found out he was selling dope for them, and owed them money.

That same year I knew a guy who tried to commit suicide. He was also in a motorcycle club, which used to be called a gang, but is now a club, because maybe Yacht Club people are Yacht Gang people. He developed a big crush on me. I met him through a friend, and we visited him a few times. He was in his 20s, and he wanted to take me to my prom. It made me uncomfortable, and we stopped visiting him.

Peter didn't become an addict in his own right until a couple years later, after we had both moved to San Francisco. I think I noticed it when he was in his early twenties. That's when he became a real creep. At holiday dinners he would criticize the food in an angry, low voice. A voice you would use to confront your abuser if you were drunk and saw them alone in a park at midnight. He would do the same thing whenever music or TV was on. There was nothing he couldn't hate with the force of a radicalized suburban kid building bombs for a terrorist operation. My parents would never ask him to leave, never insist he stop, just shake their heads and keep eating. There were three okay people at the table and one big, dark, hairy anus person. We were supposed to eat with that sharp, hostile energy shooting off of him. I could never do it. If I dated someone, Peter hated them. I don't miss that time.

Peter skips through the shallow end, then lines up a backside line over the death box. I am so amped from his run that I juice it a little harder than I had been before, and go frontside over the light, but come out farther than I expected, and clip my front wheel on the bottom step of the ladder. I fly off my board and land really hard on my left hip, whacking my head quickly. I lie on the bottom of the pool for a minute and groan. Once he can tell I'm truly hurt, Peter walks down to help me. He grabs my hand and helps me pull myself upright. He puts his arm around my back and walks me to the stairs. I sit down.

"Do we need to go?" Peter asks.

"Just give me a few minutes," I say, with my head in my hands.

"Did you hit your head?"

"Yeah."

"You should ice it," he says. "I'm sure I can find a plastic bag around here and dig some ice out of the cooler."

Peter puts a bunch of ice into a dirty plastic grocery bag, and I sit holding it to the left side of my head. At least I didn't hit my frontal lobe. Years ago, I saw an episode of Oprah and this girl was the passenger in a car her boyfriend was driving. She wasn't wearing her seatbelt, and when they were rear-ended she flew out the front windshield and landed on the pavement, absorbing the impact with her forehead. She sustained significant damage to her frontal lobe, and then spent her life trying to have sex with her family members. They got her into playing guitar, which I'm sure was just to distract her from doing the number one best grossest thing of all time: trying to get in your parents' pants. That story is the only thing that makes me even slightly consider wearing a helmet. But I don't want to. I like the feeling of the air in my hair. That's it. I don't have a reason beyond that, and all evidence points to the fact that I should wear one. But I don't.

That night, Peter and I sit around our fire and he cooks dinner. We have a small wireless speaker playing a book on tape from my phone. We're listening to *The Lovely Bones* again. It's our third time. He really loves this book. He gave it to my mom last Christmas. You would never guess this was Peter's favorite book just by looking at him. You might think he's more likely to have a favorite bong (which he did) (but now it's mine). I really like *The Lovely Bones* too, but I like the movie even more.

I want a beer but Peter says it's a bad idea since I probably have a concussion. He wants me to set my alarm for every two hours to be sure I'm alive. Alarm goes off, I yell, "I'm alive," and we go back to sleep again. It's sweet that he's so concerned, I'm not used to him acting like he cares about anything at all.

We have to haul ass back to San Francisco because Peter is mandated by the court to attend three Narcotics Anonymous meetings a week. He's had to do this before, so I'm not convinced it's a fool-proof cure. But it's probably good, regardless. He found a meeting that's all men who were super fucked up on drugs, and one doesn't even have his left arm anymore because he ruined it shooting up. Peter's not supposed to tell me this stuff, but it makes him really giggly and he doesn't tell me names.

We make it back in time, and I drop him off at the meeting on 24th Street in the Mission. I go home to my place and drink three beers in a row, hungrily, like I've been deprived. I watch *Pretty Woman*, one of the best movies ever. I fall asleep without brushing my teeth, a beer propped on my stomach. I wake up two hours later and it's spilled all over my shirt and bed, sticky and annoying. I dump a glass of water on my bed to dilute the beer and then put a towel over it and fall back asleep.

"What up?" I text my friend Irma.

"Dude come out with me," she says, "I'll pick you up in two hours."

"Where are we going?"

"These writer kids are having a fundraiser at a sex club."

"Oh god."

"It'll be funny. Come on. It's an all-gender play party!"

"You have to buy my ticket."

"Done."

A couple hours later, Irma and I park on Market Street two blocks down from Sensations, a gay men's sex club. Normally they wouldn't let women in, but they've programmed a special night for all genders to raise money for a group of queer writers to go on tour. When we arrive, there's a registration table in the lobby. There's a heavy black curtain shielding the entrance to the club. Irma pays fifty dollars for the two of us, and then we push into the back. She's wearing black leather pants and has a ball gag tied to her belt. She's six feet tall, and unapologetically still deep in '90s sex fetishes. Her face could be read as any gender, and she half-forms the words that slop out of her mouth. She's one of those people that loves dogs so passionately that you know there is a psychic wound inside her that will never heal. We've been friends since we were seventeen, which means for about sixteen years now. There are a few guys sitting on the couches in the lobby, wearing little towels around their waists and chatting. The room could just as easily be a down-to-earth hang-out room for Lutheran teens to discuss volleyball tourneys. But the cooler of protein-heavy bodybuilding drinks, the minimal attire, and the cock drawings by a novice local artist mounted and priced on the wall tell a different story. We find stairs leading to a second floor. We walk into a glory hole maze made of thin red plywood. A few people are standing nearby. One couple is making out, while one gives the other a handjob. Another guy is using the glory holes the way god intended: to let his dong wait for a willing and anonymous sucker. I see a guy stop, appraise the dick, and decide to be of service. To our left, there are two rooms which each have a leather swing. In one, Irma's ex-girlfriend Mystique is being fisted by a butch in boxer shorts and a sports bra. She cries out loudly. We walk down a hallway to another room that set up like a fake hospital. It feels like a soap opera set from the seventies. There is a woman lying on an exam table completely naked, with a fully shaved beaver. She has several labia piercings, and it gives me a sharp shot of pain through my vagina to look at. Actually, anything painful that I see on another person's body makes pain shoot through my vagina. Especially gnarly scabs. When my grandma was alive and would get big bruises on her paper-thin skin, it would feel like a gymnast was doing a floor routine on my pelvic muscles. Anyway, a very serious masculine person attends to her with a vast menu of piercing needles. The serious needler wears a black leather vest with nothing underneath and black leather pants, and whenever she moves, there is a jingle from her waist, which is laden with chains. The room is very quiet, in great deference to this act of gravity: piercing.

I lean over to Irma and whisper, "Lifestyles." She snorts. The butch's head whips in our direction.

"Shush," they say. I get shame-faced and unable to stifle giggles. Irma grabs my arm and pulls me away.

"There's a steam room downstairs," Irma tells me.

"Is it the blowingest blow job church of all time?" I ask.

"Probably."

"Hot. Let's go."

We get downstairs and notice little cubbies where people can stash their clothes. We both decide to get naked and go in, sitting on white towels so as to protect the gateways to our interiors.

"So who's the crush who drew you to this party?" I ask Irma.

"What!"

"I know how you work."

"This girl Lila. She didn't say she's coming for sure, though. I want to hang out with you!"

"Dude, I don't care, just do your thing."

"Are you like boning anybody right now?"

"Nah. Not feeling like it."

"You're always feeling like it! You love limerence!"

"I got burned out on that a while ago."

We lean back and inhale the steam. I notice a dude let

another dude's hand slide under his towel and commence jacking him off. I inhale deeply, feeling the steam lightly burn the inside of my nose.

My brother and I are driving up to our parents' house in Calistoga for their anniversary. Weaving along Mark West Springs Road into town, I watch the manzanita branches twist around the hillside with their dark green leaves, draped with the beautiful Spanish moss that's killing the trees. The grasses and weeds are burned dark yellow, and deer graze up the embankment of one of the curves we round past the Petrified Forest. Our parents live right in town, a couple blocks off Lincoln, the main street. It is a community-theater-level suburban setting. Ranch house after ranch house flanked by lawns and rose bushes. A clear and present lack of innovation. We park in the driveway and go in through the garage, which has long been too cluttered to hold an actual car. Instead, there are bicycles, tools, cases of soda and stacks of old magazines filling the void. Inside my dad and mom are both asleep on the couch in front of the TV, which murmurs the narration to a game of golf. I find these games absurdly soothing, in a tranquil, pastoral way. A green expanse so stupid you need cacophonous abuse from the outside world to make you crave its stillness.

I sit down on the couch between my mom and dad and put my arms around them. Peter takes a photo with his phone. My mom's eyes flutter open and she hugs me. Despite our movement, my dad remains asleep. His cocktail glass is empty on the table next to him.

"Let me put dinner on," my mom says. "Or do you want to do it?" She giggles and walks away, the big joke being that we all know I'm a terrible cook.

My brother hugs my mom, then goes into the next room, which is an auxiliary family room next to the family room. He turns on another TV kinda loud. I can't tell what he's watching but there's a lot of gunfire and booming noises. I'm annoyed that he has separated himself already. I stand in the doorway and look at him while he watches the screen. He doesn't even look at me.

"You don't want to hang out with us?" I ask. He doesn't answer. To some degree, I think I've always been afraid of him. He is a tangle of mood swings and quick rage. He looks up at me, then back to the TV.

"Come sit down," he says. I walk over and sit next to him. "You *are* a tense little wombat," he says. I sit quietly and absorb the weirdness of our functioning relationship. He takes my hand and holds it. We watch violent TV until my mom calls us to eat.

I shake my dad by the shoulder to wake up and eat with us. He rips a loud snore and turns his head away from me. I shake harder until his eyes crack open and he looks around. He registers my face. He gets up and makes himself another drink.

At the dinner table we start out weirdly quiet. "So! Happy anniversary, you guys," I say. I feel like I drove a red Mini Cooper into a white brick wall at 60 mph.

"Thank you, Loma," my mom says. She sips her scotch and saws off a slice of pork chop. She's still a pretty big drinker, though not like she used to be. My parents were both big partiers when we were little, having people over most nights of the week and playing their records loudly in the living room. I hated it at the time, but in retrospect it seems cool that they didn't let kids change their lives too much.

One of their friends, a neighbor, molested my brother for

years. Peter started wetting his bed and having nightmares. It went on for two years before the guy's wife caught him. She kicked him out, and told my parents but it didn't make anything better. Peter went into counseling at a local church that we didn't even attend. I never understood how that happened. My dad just started drinking more. He was sullen and spent a lot of time in the garage watching TV, not talking to any of us. My mom pulled back on her drinking and stopped having people over all the time. Peter seemed so sad and alone. I wanted to make him feel better but didn't know how. He got angry easily and threw fits all the time, and that made me uncomfortable. Hating my wounded brother made me feel like a monster, but I didn't like how everything would stop the moment he got upset. If we were going out for pizza and he didn't like his shoes, it would take half an hour of him yelling and crying, and my mom struggling with him while my dad stayed silent until she would finally let him wear his slippers out and we could get pizza, which had lost a lot of its shine by then.

I make myself ask my dad how he's doing. He answers in his customarily brief manner: "Good." I feel like I'm part of a procedure. Arrive, greet, sit down, eat one bite at a time. I thought this shit was supposed to be about human connection. I know there are families out there who talk to each other and play board games. I saw Glenn Close on Letterman one time talking about her boyfriend's family, and how they wore sumo suits and wrestled each other at Thanksgiving. She said they were really fun people. I wanted a playful family of my own.

Peter's phone rings.

"Pete," my dad starts.

"One second," Peter says, holding his finger up and backing up his chair. He disappears into the bathroom.

"So, how's your job hunt?" My mom asks me.

"I'm doing some babysitting here and there," I say. "I was thinking I should look into trade school, maybe like plumbing or electrical. Something that pays well, and eventually I can start my own business and make my own schedule."

"You want to spend your time in other people's shit?" my dad asks.

"I already do psychically, so why not?"

"Well, you're being funny, but it's tough work. You wouldn't believe how some people live."

"There's a chance I would believe it."

"Can you afford trade school, honey?" my mom asks.

"I don't know. It's probably a few thousand dollars or something."

"I was talking to Sylvia Hernandez last week and she said her daughter Jenny was shocked at the cost of beauty school. It sounded like it was over ten thousand dollars."

"Gonna be a tough climb for you, Paloma," my dad says. "You're aimless, and you have a problem with authority."

"Thanks for the fucking support, Dad," I say. I drop my fork on my plate and it clatters loudly.

"Am I wrong?"

"Are you confusing this commentary with parenting?" I shout and push my chair back. Peter comes back in and tries to assess what's going on.

"Hey, do you mind if we head back to San Francisco kinda soon?"

"Not at all," I blurt angrily. I look at my mom, who looks down at her lap. My brother walks over to her and gives her a hug from behind, as she sits. He walks over and shakes my dad's hand. I squeeze my mom's shoulder, and walk out.

When we're back on the road, driving through the inky

dark, I blink back a few waves of tears. "So who was on the phone?" I ask Peter.

"Oliver. He's in the Shitty," he says.

"Good one," I say. Peter loves calling The City the "Shitty."

"We're going to hook up when we get back."

"Where is he living now?"

"Humboldt County. He's couch surfing."

"He still shooting dope?"

My brother doesn't answer for a while. He stares at the road, and I unreasonably want to scold him severely for making me wait for the answer.

"Probably," he says finally.

I'm lying in bed back in San Francisco, grumpy as fuck after dealing with my family. My neck hurts and it feels like my left hip is tight. I don't even know why, though probably from a skateboarding fall. I need to snap out of it, so I try to remember if I've ever thought anything was funny. Everything feels so powerfully stupid right now. I know I've seen some funny things on TV. I remember watching a Gallagher comedy special over and over when I was a kid. It must have been on HBO or something, and I thought it was the funniest thing of all time. I've watched it since, and of course it's all outrageously sexist, childish humor. But man, the guy was clearly enjoying himself. So what difference did it make to him?

What if I went through life as a truly mediocre stand-up comedian? I start giggling to myself. I mean, what if I had no idea that I was bad at it and found easy satisfaction attending open mics and delivering flat jokes to lukewarm reception? It sounds glorious to have no shame or standards.

I start thinking about what I would do onstage. Maybe

I could market myself as a gardener/comedian, the dumbest combo ever. I could wear white Dickies and a white T-shirt with dirt smudges all over them. Maybe some grass stains. A belt full of gardening tools. Maybe a ball cap with the bill pushed up.

"Good evening, I'm Paloma, thanks everybody for coming. I have a question for you. Why is it I can pull weeds out of the ground all day but I can't *weed* the jerks out of my life? Maybe I should *smoke* some *grass* and figure it out."

A couple small titters from the crowd.

"I'm just another jerk with a weed whip. I'll come trim your hedges but if we really get down to business and I mean like fucking, you'll notice I'm gardener in the streets, hair farmer in the sheets. Full bush on my downstairs! Pubes without borders!"

That one might be hard for people to believe because actually, I am largely hairless. But I think it's funny.

"I know this isn't going to be a popular idea but I want to cultivate a secondary full bush out of my butt. I want a giant burst of wiry, filthy hair tufting out of my buns. I then want to trim it into a flat top. Straight buzz cut of the butt. It will look like I have a paintbrush wedged in there or a Dolph Lundgren doll whose feet are wreaking havoc on my tender anal interior." Because this material directs so much attention to my ass I would have to decide if it's better to wear flattering white pants or dumpy ones. Does my self-deception also include delusions about my appearance?

"Why is it that so many women who sport a full bush have shaved heads? Isn't there some kind of policy regarding even distribution of hair?" I wonder if I should find a way to use the word "hirsute" here. It's such a good word. "I know there is a public idea of Lesbian Hairstyle Choices. Short up on your head, unruly on the V, is clearly a staple of gay lady hair. This is what I have learned from pantsing lesbians. I'd like to see the day that hairstyles are fully disconnected from gender. But more than that, I think I'd just like the idea of a gender binary abolished." Zing them with an unexpected deep and/or political thought!!

"Why the hell do so many people plant roses? You can get the biggest weirdo, the person who has to research obscure music and thrift bizarre clothes and get novelty coffee mugs, but when you do their garden, they will invariably pick the most generic plants in the whole world, and want them placed in an artless and rudimentary manner. It will be roses and boxwood all the way." Too niche? Impossible. Do you think Gallagher ever felt like he needed to get less specific? I don't.

"Why do the richest people take the longest time to pay their bills? And why do they fight their charges more than anyone else?" Wait what is the joke here. "Do you think they just can't see their bills through all the caviar, Bentleys, ivory figurines, Manolos, Pepperidge Farm Mint Milano cookies, pet jaguars, orchids, vacation home horse farms in Argentina, private jets and blowhards? I wonder if bills for rich people are like human turds in my driveway are for me? Ignore them at first, then hose them down half-heartedly trying not to splash in my face, do an okay job, move on.

"The key is to live like you mean to. Be the hoe you want to dig in the dirt. Keep the raccoons away and call everything that thrives in spite of you what it is: a weed."

Good night! A career is born. I walk offstage, victorious. I drive home in a beige Toyota Camry. I drink a glass of water and eat a day-old blueberry muffin. Life is mellow and I'm content.

My brother and I are meeting for coffee at a place at Al-abama and 21st. He says he has "a proposition" he wants to run by me. I can't imagine what that could mean. It sounds like the kind of meeting ladies have where they decide to lose weight together. I come in and see him sitting on the back patio with a coffee. I grab one and walk out into the bright, overcast day.

"Loma!" He says, cheery as can be. "I was going to buy you coffee."

"Beat you to it."

"So, how's it going?"

"What? Normal. Why?"

"Have you found a job?"

"Are you serious? Did Mom tell you to ask me that?"

"I have some really cool shit happening right now," he says with uncharacteristic excitement. "Oliver is helping a couple guys I know start a trim house in Mendo. I'm gonna run it. I mean I'm one of the people running it."

"Oh. Okay," I say, as flat as I can. What a stupid piece of news.

"This isn't just a farm, we're specifically being commis-sioned by some famous people whose names I can't say here. It's a big deal. We're going to be growing the best product in California, probably the country."

"Weed is legal. Why don't they have an assistant get a card and buy their shit like everyone else does?"

"Tabloids. They don't want the attention."

"Snoop Dogg and Seth Rogen don't seem to have an issue."

"Yeah but it's their image and their management is down with that."

"I thought you hated celebrities."

"If they want to pay me, no judgment. Especially if they want to back up the money truck like they're doing now. Oliver and Rigo have been planning this out for the last six months. It's gonna be tight."

Rigo is one of Pete's best friends who he met in jail a few years ago. I'm not entirely clear on why Pete was in there. Seems like it was probably a minor possession bust for heroin or something. I'm the only one in our family who has any enthusiasm for details. I asked my mom and dad what happened this time and they just waved me off, fatigued about the whole thing. Who can blame them? My brother and I are such embarrassments. They would never, ever say that but I know we are. Their friends' kids did the old-fashioned stuff like getting married young, having kids, and working anachronistic jobs like banker and real estate agent. Things that still pay well and carry a level of stability and prestige with people my parents' age. Then there's me and Peter, just dicking around and trying to be "happy." My great-grandfather worked on the railroad laying ties and busted his body to raise a huge litter of kids alone and give his descendants a new life in this country. If we're building on that, then it's in a real lateral way. Maybe more of a spiritually seeking, downwardly mobile way. Which is hard to value when I think about the brutal physical labor of the railroad. We're just the privileged douches of our generation. Comfortably useless, desperate to be high, terrified to feel anything yet hoping to bond with another human being, valuing animals over people, recycling. I don't buy organic anything though, I think that stuff is baloney. I think of my dad, languishing in his permanent divot in the couch, napping next to a fleet of pills meant to deal with supposed chronic pain. He was laid off in his early fifties by Sundial, a small software company he helped build that couldn't afford him because the CEO was supporting a few not-so-secret (except from his wife) boyfriends he had scattered through Silicon Valley. I dare anyone to see my dad's ongoing emotional k-hole and still think a straight job is any kind of guarantee, or that hard work pays off.

Rigo was in the clink for beating his girlfriend. I hold this against him. I know he's a repository of secrets about my brother, most of which I'm sure I'm glad I don't know. Dudes really bond in a special way over their abject shittiness. I suppose life's donkey moments deserve companionship. I like that Peter has Rigo because he needs a friend who is close to him. But I don't think they get into the best shit together.

"Hey have you ever thought about what you would do if you died?" Peter abruptly asks. "If I died I would cold kick it with Grandpa Kai all the time. We would go bass fishing in Canada, like in remote lakes where no one visits. Wildlife of all kinds wandering around and not scared of us. Blue skies, clouds, whatever, I wouldn't care."

"I would sit next to a waterfall with Joni Mitchell and sing all day and then eat nachos and skate a pool."

"I'll skate the pool with you."

"Cool."

"But let's wait a long time until we die," he says.

"But not too long, because I don't want to ever feel trapped in my body and just waiting to die. I don't want to live past seventy-five, eighty tops."

"Me neither."

"So why am I here with you talking about your big awesome trim job?"

"I almost forgot! We need someone who can be an actual liaison. Take product to Los Angeles and present to our clients. You'd have to trim for a month first though, just to get to know the plants. Actually, I should just let Rigo tell you about the job."

"What's the pay?"

"More than you've ever made. Like four hundred a day to trim, more to transport and sell."

"This is so fucking cool!" I yell, and reach out to high-five him, like the dork I am. A warm wash rolls over my body. I imagine using a machete to lop the top off a giant bottle of champagne. I have no particular passion for or against marijuana but if it means good money, I am fully onboard to be the new pothead in town.

There's a knock at my bedroom door and Pete pokes his head in. He stayed over last night so we could watch movies.

"How are you doing, my dude?" I wipe my eyes and pull my comforter up. "Come sit." He climbs on my bed and leans against the wall.

"I'm good."

"Did you sleep well?"

"Your couch is amazing. It's like sleeping in a pile of creamed corn."

"Yummy."

"I'm so stoked we're going to work together."

"Me too. Do any women work there?"

"Trim crew is all women. They're better at it and easier to work with.

"You'll get no arguments from me on that," I say.

"I've heard a couple bad stories though."

"What do you mean?"

"I heard a place north of us was robbed and the guys kidnapped one of the trimmers. Kept her hostage, did fucked-up shit. Cops found her dead."

"Ew, ew, don't tell me shit like that! I won't be able to get it out of my head until the day I die peacefully in my sleep. Do you guys have security?"

"It's not necessary, we're super remote. There's not even really a driveway up to the farm. You have to have an off-road vehicle to get up there."

"I see," I say, fighting off images of the kidnapped lady.

"So what are we doing tonight?" he asks.

"I don't know, let me think about it."

"Cool if I use your computer?"

"Yeah. Put on some coffee, okay?"

That night we drive to a bar. We're both silent, staring off into the foggy night and thinking.

"Wait, how was seeing Oliver?" I ask.

"So good."

"How did he seem? Like, drug-wise?"

"He's trying to get it under control, especially with this big opportunity. He had to tell the crew he was going to quit. Which has to be pronto if we're heading up next week."

"Do you think he can swing that?"

"Hope so."

We're going to meet Irma and Oliver at this bar called The Wreck Room where our friend's soft rock cover band is playing. I park on Mission Street, and we walk up to the bar. There's a guy with a very pronounced brow, kind of troglo- dyte-looking, checking IDs. He stares at my picture, then up at me, then back down, like I would want to scam my way into this crappy bar.

"This you?"

"Yes."

"How old are you?"

"Thirty-two."

"This isn't you, this looks like your older sister."

"I don't even have a sister. Can I go in?"

"This isn't your sister?" He points at Irma.

"I think you're just detecting a general gayness among us."

He waves us inside.

We walk into the bar, which is long and narrow, and impossibly dark. As we get near the back, I see there's a slightly wider area with tables and chairs, and a small stage. The people in Smooth Nites always look like the '80s spilled all over them from a giant paint can. I see Donna, the lead singer, who has huge, black crimped hair and a black dress with a billowing white ruffle extending from her right shoulder to her left hip. She looks unstable in the best way. Then there's Bob, who sings with Donna. He's in faded pegged jeans and a turquoise tank top with big armholes and a cartoon of a surfer on the front. It says "Totally Tubular!" which I like a lot. The best is how the people of Smooth Nites always give 110% when they're performing. There is the visual goofballery of their clothes but the music is well played.

I see Irma down the bar, drinking a pint of beer and talking with an older guy in a fedora and a Grateful Dead T-shirt. Not super-old, maybe like mid-fifties. It seems kind of random, but what do I know about her life, really? She's one of those people who will mention to me that she's been seeing a girl for six months and it will be the first I've heard of it, even though she calls me her best friend and we see each all the time. I don't mind.

Wait, maybe the fedora guy is the hot tub guy. She told me there's a man who she meets at The Wreck Room for drinks then goes back to his house to sit in his hot tub. He always has piles of coke and speed sitting out on a table. Anyone is welcome to the hot tub and the drugs, provided they are naked and female. Any kind of female can plop down on his leather couch and have at it. He also has various vintage guitars that Irma can play. He says he loves seeing her small woman fingers on them. What is the feeling when he sees them? Small fingers strumming, little digits pushing the strings down. Woman. Sex. Orgasm. Wanting. Distance. Rejection. Irma told me about this guy a couple months ago, casually, over giant hamburgers made from pure organic beef at Joe Grinds His Own. I had a huge iced tea in front of me and a pile of seemingly never-ending French fries.

"He's cool," she said.

"What's his name?"

"Jared."

"Oh."

"He never tries anything with me."

"Oh. I guess that's good."

"Yeah. It's really good. Because who knows what I would do, I might just do it with him."

"Really?"

"Sure."

"What would you get out of it?"

She shrugs her shoulders. "Coke."

"Why do you keep this stuff secret from me?"

"I'm telling you right now."

"Yeah, but you've been doing it for months."

"So?"

"How come you never invite me?" I asked this even though I'm so glad I've never been part of these nights.

"Really? Why don't I bring you on my gross drug adventures? God, how horrifying. I never want you to see me that way. I'm an ugly person at four in the morning when there's not enough cocaine to go around. God. I will never bring you with me."

I felt satisfied with her explanation, and then kinda lonely. How stupid. How can I feel left out of something I don't want to be part of?

Peter orders us drinks and pays for them. This seems wildly generous. We walk down to the end of the bar, sliding past people in the narrow space between the barstools and the wall. Irma and Peter hug. Irma is kind of a sister to Pete too. She's been coming to our family functions and hanging out with Pete the whole time we've known each other.

"What up," I hear behind me, and turn to see Oliver clapping hands with Peter. He turns to me and smiles. "Paloma, what up girl, it's been a minute." His eyes are pinpoints in toilet water. High as hell. I wonder if he's going full speed on dope since he knows he has to quit soon. My uncle used to be like this.

Smooth Nites is about to start, so we stand at the back of the small crowd. Bob and Donna launch into "Always," that old duet by Atlantic Starr, which I love. I sing with them at the top of my lungs. I'm not the best singer in the world, kind of perpetually flat, but you have to admit that anyone who loves to sing makes up for lack of skill with enthusiasm. It's the whole principle behind karaoke. I look over at Pete and he has a small smile on his lips, and his arm around Irma. He looks happy. That makes me happy. Something inside me relaxes.

Next they sing the theme song from the movie *The Never-Ending Story*. Now people all over the room are singing as loud as possible and I run to the front of the stage, popping veins in my face from singing so hard (just saying that for drama, no veins actually burst). After a few exhilarating minutes I walk back to Irma and Peter. Oliver is missing. My tiny bladder kicks in and I head for the bathroom, which miraculously has no line, probably because the band is playing. Just as I'm pushing the door open I notice Oliver in the corner, leaning against the wall and nodding out. I walk over and touch his arm.

"Oliver." No answer. I shake him lightly. "Ollie, you should probably go home." His eyes open the smallest bit. He shifts his weight.

"I don't really have a place right now," he says.

"Where've you been staying?"

"Got kicked out."

Through a heavy panel of dread I say, "Do you want to stay at my house? You can take my keys and we'll meet you back there later." I feel intense panic, but swallow it, and hand him my keys. It would be wrong not to help someone without a place to stay. Especially a sad idiot like this. He pats my shoulder in a totally stupid way, and leaves.

I walk back out onto the floor where they're playing "Hard Habit to Break" by Chicago. Everyone is singing along loudly and swaying together. After the song ends, Irma and I get more drinks. We end up closing the bar. I dance so hard I think I break my little toe from ramming into some guy.

We tumble outside and hang around talking and smoking until Peter wants to go. I can't believe he's put up with all the drinking and idiocy while sober. It has to be powerfully annoying. We say goodnight to Irma and walk down the street to my car. I puff on a wet-dirty-sweat-sock-tasting cigarette.

"Can you drive us?" Peter asks, then gets a mischievous smile. "Just kidding, ya drunkard!"

"Will you stay over again? Oliver is there and I'm a little freaked out by that."

"What do you mean, he's there?"

"He didn't have a place to stay so I said he could go hang out. He was nodding out at the bar."

"He's been at the Eula, why didn't he just go there?" The Eula is a residential hotel on 16th Street.

"He told me he was kicked out of wherever he was."

"Really? Okay."

A few minutes later we walk up to my front door and knock. No answer. Peter doesn't have a key to my place and Oliver has mine so we're locked out. I hit the doorbell several times, no answer. Peter calls Oliver's Tracfone, or whatever those phones are called that you pay as you go. No answer. My landlord lives upstairs, and I would rather not bug him at two in the morning, so Peter and I go to his place and crash.

I wake up on Peter's old olive green couch at five in the morning, booze sweaty and disgusting, my clothes from the night before twisted around my body. I'm obscenely dehydrated. I get a glass of water and stare at the filthy sink full of dishes. Half an hour later my brother wakes up.

"What the hell are you doing up?"

"Can't sleep lately. Anxiety."

"Probably the whole being sober thing, right?"

"Guess so."

"I hope Oliver is okay."

"Want to go over? Is your landlord up?"

"I'll text him. I tried Oliver but no answer."

We meet my landlord at my house and he lets us in. I check my bedroom and no Oliver. We get to the living room and there he is, on the couch. His face is a greyish-blue, and his rig lies next to him on top of his backpack.

"Fuck, call 911!" I holler at my brother, who is right next to me.

"Calm down, I'm on it."

"I'm not going to fucking calm down! This isn't a time for calm! Don't tell me to see a dead person and mellow out!" I start yelling and Peter walks out of the room, giving an address to the operator. I try to find a pulse in Oliver's neck, even though I think he's gone. We wait. I feel like throwing up. I go into the bathroom and sit on the tub next to the toilet trying to throw up. A little bit comes out but nothing much. Just searing nausea in my abdomen. We leave the front door open so when the ambulance arrives they walk right in and to Oliver. They attempt CPR, but to no avail. He's gone. He's in my house. We're just bodies in space.

Peter deals with the steps of calling Oliver's mom, a sad alcoholic lady in Virginia with violent boyfriends and a smattering of other kids from volatile men. Oliver had a raw deal the whole way. I start walking through the Mission. I go all the way down Capp Street, then up 16th Street to Valencia and over to Market. I keep a good pace. People hang out, play chess, pee on the sidewalk. I cut up Hyde Street, jog over on Pine, taking on some punishing hills. I finally arrive in Chinatown and land at a vegetarian restaurant on Washington Street called The Lucky Creation. I order a plate of noodles with fake chicken. I decide to try to be in the restaurant purely as an observer, receiving information without judgment. Watching, feeling. The fluorescent lights make it feel like an office, like there should be a bunch of people talking about a TV show around a fax machine. A couple eats across from me, not speaking to each other, slurping. There are Germans at another table mulling over the menu. A lady sits at the cash register watching everyone, then looking out the door. I stay for a while and drink a lot of green tea. I start the walk home. Now it seems long and terrible. I try to get back in observer mode and just let it happen.

I don't hear from Peter for a few days. He doesn't hear from me either. I half-assedly look for a job, but hope that the pot farm work is still mine. I don't know why it feels like there's a rift between me and my brother. I feel like I fucked up when I didn't do anything but witness Oliver's dead body with him. I don't know how to explain it. After three days I text Peter.

"Hey dude." No answer.

"You okay?" No answer.

Two hours later, I try one more time. "Are we still going to Mendo next week for work or what?"

I see that he's writing me back. Then the little dots go away. They start, then stop. Ten minutes later I get the text, "Yeah still on."

"Want to get dinner?" I write. No answer.

We're supposed to leave in four days. I walk over to Peter's house and knock. I text him "I'm outside," and he texts back "Okay." A few minutes later, he finally opens the door. Immediately I can tell his vibe is off. He is sour and sharp, and his eyes look a million miles away.

"Dude, I've been worried about you," I say.

"Why?"

"Because I haven't heard from you since Oliver. That was really gnarly."

"What do you want from me?"

"Why are you being like this?" I plead, and he starts closing the door on me. "Please stop!" I say and put my foot in to block it. He pushes my foot out with his own, but leaves the door cracked.

"We're leaving on Tuesday," he says.

"Okay."

"I have a lot of shit to do between now and then. I'll text you."

I sigh and leave. His sour mood is so demoralizing. I wish there was a way to guarantee he would stop acting like this forever. I call Irma to see what she's up to.

"Hey, good morning, pal!" Irma is bright and energetic.

"What are you doing today?"

"Wanna come with me to walk my dogs? Bernal Hill? Maybe we get a drink after or something."

"Yes. Two-thirty?"

"See ya!"

I drive down Cesar Chavez and make a right on Alabama. It occurs to me, apropos of nothing, that it would be hilarious to pick up a couple four-packs of wine coolers and bring them up the hill for me and Irma. I stop at the corner store on Precita and Alabama and walk in to a cloud of incense. There's a big teenage girl sitting on a stool, talking on her cell phone. She doesn't look at me. She's wearing a grey hoodie and jeans that wrinkle up all over her like small waves. There's a deli case across from the checkout, and a few meats and cheeses are strewn about, not filling the space, and looking a little past their eat-by date. Food poisoning waiting to happen. I walk back through the shelves of cat food and laundry detergent and Chunky Soup to the coolers and pull out a pack of pink bottles and a pack of green ones. Strawberry and green apple wine coolers. The gold foil wrapped around the tops of the bottles really has a top-shelf feel.

I pay the girl on the cell phone who only stops her conversation long enough to ask for $6.86. She has sweet, dark brown eyes and eyelashes that curl up to her eyebrows. I've been stopping here for years. The girl's family moved to San Francisco from Eritrea years ago and took over the store from another family. She's been working here since she was a little kid. I drive to the top of the hill and park in a short row of pick-up trucks. I see several dog walkers and their crews. The dogs wander around, peeing, and sniffing, and greeting other dogs. A beautiful grey and black Great Dane lopes by. I like standing on this mound of nature planted in the urban landscape.

"Yo!" Irma hollers and strides toward me, a pack of dogs jetting away from her like sparks. She carries a long red Chuck-It over one shoulder, that long flexible plastic arm that helps you throw tennis balls super far. A huge ring of keys is hanging from a loop on her black jeans. Irma is one of those women who was born with instant muscles. She's shaped like a prehistoric man. Even if she eats pepperoni pizza for every meal and drinks only beer she has broad shoulders, thick arms, and these legs that make her look like a Roman athlete from long ago, wavy with muscle. I just want to put a discus in her hand and send her to work.

I direct our path up the hill, lugging the paper bag full of wine coolers, which bumps against my leg rhythmically. The dogs wander and play and get acquainted with each other's genitals. At the top of the road we climb over a steel railing onto a flat area where we can see the city sprawl north to downtown, east to the Bay and Oakland, and south to Portola Valley, Visitacion Valley and the Excelsior. We sit on a rock and watch the animals and people.

"What's in the bag?"

"A flavor sensation." I pull out the wine coolers and lay a cold, pink bottle in Irma's open hand.

"Aren't these illegal? Or like illegal in Europe because they're so flammable?"

"That's UltraSport, dummy." I crack mine open and shake my head as I gulp the impossibly sweet and bubbly wine cooler. Irma pulls the cap off her bottle, throws it into the grass, and takes a long swallow.

"Dude!" I slap her arm.

"What?"

"Littering!"

"When did you turn into an environmentalist?"

"I've always cared about this!"

"Live with it, sister."

Irma stands up and secures a tennis ball with the Chuck-It. She cranks her arm back and and sends the fuzzy green orb sailing, setting five dogs sprinting after it. A compact Jack Russell runs back with the ball in his mouth and stands panting with the other dogs, waiting for another throw. Irma repeatedly wings the ball and the animals chase farther and farther across the top of Bernal Hill. There's something comical about all the exertion and joy happening in front of me, the superlative throws, and running, and response for the love of the air and the earth. I open a second wine cooler and sip more of its addictive sugar. My body, once I get a taste of sweetness, craves it in junkie proportions.

A woman walks up to us and looks at Irma.

"I think I saw you throw this bottle cap."

"So what?" Irma snaps.

"I saw you throw this on the ground and I'm bringing it over here because we don't want litter on Bernal Hill."

"Who is 'we'?"

"The people who live here."

"I live here. Who exactly are you speaking for?"

"A very tight-knit group of us who are dedicated to making Bernal a nice place to live. Do you like living in a messy neighborhood?"

"Bernal Hill wasn't always uptight, you know. You fucking people and your rules for perfect liberal living. It's creepy."

"I'm not trying to be uptight. . . ."

"But you are. So go away."

The woman keeps the bottle cap in her hand and walks away, looking glum.

"You hurt her very rarefied feelings. Why were you such a jerk?" I ask Irma.

"I get sick of the weird passive-aggressive snottiness of this neighborhood sometimes."

"Good point. You ready for another wine cooler?"

"Just a second, I want to throw the ball for these goofballs one more time. What do you want to do after we drop the dogs off?"

"Let's go to Pier 39 and look at the seals."

"In-town tourism!"

"I love doing the stuff that normal people do."

"I know, me too, it feels so perverted."

"No giving tourists good directions. Only bad information is allowed."

"Deal."

I park my car back at Irma's house. Irma unloads her animals then picks me up and we make our way to the other side of town in her van, an '85 Chevy full-size, dark brown with a big tan stripe around the middle. I love vans. A little house on wheels, the vehicle for adventure. Irma drives like she believes a power greater than herself is protecting her, cutting other cars off, grazing indignant pedestrians, running over the curb at almost every turn. She barely notices the honking and fear of people who thought our civic code and local laws meant something. I can't tell what in the hell she is focusing on that mutes her senses so effectively. She can't just be excited to see the seals, that doesn't make sense. We've seen them a million times. Maybe it's a low-grade form of astral projection that leaves her physically here, but otherwise wholly elsewhere, the kind of thing that would take training in another person and comes naturally due to trauma in others. We park on Francisco Street, kind of close to North Beach, and walk toward the Bay and the most cheeseball tourist part of town. I love a tourist zone, it feels like walking through an actual cartoon.

It's a bright day though there are clouds in the sky. I carry a green apple wine cooler in my right hand and drink it while we walk. When we cross the street to Pier 39 there's a group of tourists standing a few yards away from a classic Pier 39 entertainer. The Bush Guy. He hides behind a four-foot-high bush, which is actually just a big, leafy branch he's holding, and jumps out and scares people walking by as he yells "Gotcha!" Once you've been a victim of his sport, it's the next best thing to stand by and watch it happen to others. We pass the onlookers and their smart walking shoes and then we pass another entertainer, a guy painted entirely silver. He stands still on a milk crate, waiting for a tip to bust some dance moves. I throw a dollar into his jar but keep walking. Normally I would stop and watch him do his thing. But the seals are waiting for us. We walk down the planks of the deck that lead to the cove where the seals sun themselves on large wooden squares floating in the sea water. The seals rest in giant shiny grey piles, pushed up against each other, flippers against their sides. Every now and then one dives into the brine and swims around. We watch a seal launch itself out of the water onto one of the floating squares and try to lie down, except another seal won't let him. The seal who was already there barks angrily at the visitor, they bump necks, and the uninvited seal slides back into the water, then pops up at another deck where he has better luck.

"Want to go to Jay's House of Blues?" Irma loops her arm through mine. We set off down the walkway toward the land of bread bowls dripping with clam chowder and American music.

The inside of Jay's is just enough of an enclosure to be considered "inside." The wood of the walls is thin and cheap, and it's covered with white paint that's been stained with fingerprints and grease and, at least psychically, cheesy blues. I don't actually know anything about blues music, maybe this is the unlikely bastion of the best. There are wide windows open to the street and flies zoom around in their box-shaped flight plans. How do they turn such perfect right angles?

We sit down at a table with a large line drawing of Muddy Waters shellacked beneath its surface. A surfer-looking guy walks up to take our order. He swings his chin-length black hair off his face to look at us and keeps his head tilted back a tiny bit to maintain the view.

"Hello ladies. Can I get you started with something to drink?"

"Yeah alright, let's have whatever your biggest drink is, like one of those things for two people," says Irma.

"The scorpion bowl?"

"Yeah and can we have it with no ice?"

"I'm gonna have to ask my manager. I don't want to be a douche but I could get in trouble for doing that because without ice, it's a lot more alcohol."

He leaves and I look at Irma. She's watching our waiter walk away.

"Walk away slow, right? What an ass. I wish I could have little man hips like that. Look at that! Being shaped like a woman with these bullshit hips and tits is the biggest insult, the most cruel of all facts beyond my control."

"Maybe you should try running or biking, I think they pare down the ole hips."

"Yeah but if I do that I run the risk of losing weight and revealing a waist underneath my spare tire. Then I'll really look like a lady. I have this fear that I'm an hourglass under this stuff." Irma grabs a fistful of her cute belly chub. "At least now I'm more like a tube, same width from shoulders to hips. That's way more manly than being skinny and curvy. The kind of ladies I want to pork don't like guys like me to be thin or ladylike, it's just the facts."

"Ew, 'pork.'"

Our waiter walks up with a sad look that seems like a caricature. "You guys, I'm sorry, my manager says that if you have a scorpion bowl without the ice they have to make it with less booze, or if you want the full glass you have to pay thirty bucks instead of eighteen."

"Amazingly lame," Irma says and I can tell she's holding back a longer string of insults. Her lips are pressed together and her nostrils are flared.

"So do you guys still want one?"

"Yeah and you can just make it regular, with the ice," I try to intercept before things get stupid way too early in the day.

We drink our scorpion bowl, and there's the cheesy moment of us each having straws in the same drink and sipping it together. Irma stares down into the bowl, watching the liquid sink down the side of the glass and roll up her straw. I look at her and wonder how she can be so annoying and so perfect at the same time. All the sweet blue drink is gone and Irma flips her straw away.

"That was stupid. Let's get another." She spins around and waves at the waiter. "Hey, dude, ask your manager if we can pay you eighteen bucks to give us another drink that costs about a buck fifty to make. See if he thinks he has time."

Our surfer boy leans in and talks to the bartender, hopefully not telling him to spit in our drink. He brings the second glowing blue mini toxic ocean over to our table and sets it down, then cocks his head back and looks at us. He has these soft, full lips that I'm really into. They are a deep bluish pink and I want to feel them where my jaw meets my neck. "I'm not trying to be an asshole you guys, like about checking with my boss or whatever. I'd rather give you all the drinks you want for free."

"It's cool," I start to say, but Irma talks over me.

"Yeah, whatever to make a buck, right? It's like whatever, okay man, fifty dollars later we've had the equivalent of two shots each and I think it's bullshit. Maybe you should think about the fact that you're working at a place that screws people over and that makes you part of the problem. You have a choice, and you choose to help the hand of injustice. It's pretty lame."

"Well aren't you feeding the machine if you spend your money here? You could get drinks somewhere else." He looks at her like he's peeking over a wall. His hands on his waist.

"There's nowhere else to go down here! God! You had us over a barrel. We can go somewhere else in a nicer neighborhood for less money, I bet. And you can tell your manager it was your idea."

I start laughing at her and sipping the bowl and maybe

I take a little more than my share, which isn't hard when it's mostly ice.

"Gimme that thing," Irma reaches across the table, sloshes a good three dollars worth out of the glass and puts it directly under her face and drinks down the rest. I'm getting a little ramped up. This is that feeling when I start methodically tossing all my rules out the window and it's a little hard to hang on to who I am in my head but I roll with it.

We walk up the sidewalk past a souvenir shop full of postcards and shot glasses and coffee mugs with trolleys on them. The height of camp. Ubiquitous "Alcatraz Swim Team" T-shirts droop on plastic hangers and a small cluster of snow globes stands on a card table. A few people poke around in the store to find the thing that will help them remember their trip. It's strange to see all of this memorabilia meant to define San Francisco for those who don't live here. Not a single one of these items describes the city I know. My world is punk rock, gay people, skateboarding. What these people would consider the fringes. My life never feels like the margins to me. Does any local feel like the Golden Gate Bridge and Alcatraz define their life here? I suppose if you're indigenous and spend Thanksgiving at sunrise ceremonies on Alcatraz, that would be a part of your world. I don't know, it's too much to consider. I'm not an academic.

We continue on toward the van. We pass a guy sitting in a driveway, a big black jacket covering him, jeans and crappy high tops too, bent over and nodding off. One of his arms is in a cast. He has thin, dirty hair and a red scalp. I hate seeing that. But with a few drinks in me I can push his image out of my mind with ease. I love the twilight hours. A flock of wild parrots flies over us squeaking and chirping. My dad bought parakeets when I was in high school and they stayed in this little gold cage with the door wired open. One of the most beautiful and most surreal feelings of my life was taking a nap on the couch in the living room and hearing them fly above me in a half-dream state. The soft and rushed flutter of their wings held a secret about time and space.

We slog down Columbus Avenue toward Irma's van. For a flash I think we shouldn't drive owing to drunkenness. But buses seem inconvenient and cabs too expensive so I decide to hope that we don't kill anyone, as technically this is not the first time we've been women under the influence driving, and we haven't hurt anyone yet.

"Where are we going?" I ask, not ready to end the night.

"Let's go to my place," Irma says and rips out a huge burp. "Oh yeah." It happens again. "Aw fuck, that one fizzed out my fuckin' nose. Dude. Weirdest feeling." Irma paws at her nose then yanks the car into drive and we jump forward on our way back to her house nestled in the back of Bernal Hill.

We sail along the Embarcadero with all its bright lights and smooth pavement. The Bay rolls and sparkles in greater darkness to our left. When Irma is sober she runs over every corner and terrorizes humanity but now that her brain is scrambled she has laser-like focus. We take a left onto Third Street and cross the bridge, passing the ballpark and entering the rapidly transforming nowhere of China Basin. A little biotech here and some university offshoots there, street cleaning and parking lots, next thing you know your wide-open space is owned and maintained by effective profiteers and you're left with that old friend nostalgia kissing you like a sister.

We cut up Jerrold Street. Honestly, this is not a fast or reasonable way home, but we'll get there. When we finally pull up in front of Irma's house on Franconia Street she blasts her foot down on the brake and throws the van into park. I lurch forward and catch myself with both hands on the dashboard.

"Put your car in 'park,' parking brake *on*!" Irma zings the parking brake to the floor. "Shots!" She busts her door open with her foot and runs around the van to let me out. Not because my door won't open—it will—but in a gesture of comic chivalry. She grabs my hand and says, "Madame" as I dismount so I laugh and kiss her on the cheek. She keeps hold of my hand and backs me up against the chain-link fence between us and the freeway.

"You're sexier than all the strippers I know," Irma says in a husky voice, unexpectedly earnest. It seems like such a dude thing to say.

"Man, you must be wasted," I say and push her away lightly in the chest. She lets her arms drop heavily to her sides and steps back, looking at me through the hair hanging in her eyes.

"Yeah, but my brain is real and my heart is true," she says with wide hambone eyes and points one finger like a gun at her brain and one like a gun at her heart. "I know what I'm saying."

"You and all the drunks on Capp Street. Holy crap," I say and turn around and walk toward her house. For the hell of it I run to her front door and slam into it like I didn't know it would be there. I dramatically fall to the doormat in what I hope looks like a heap of limbs. Gilda Radner as Roseanne Roseannadanna. I relax then somehow I hoist my bones to vertical. Irma lifts the doormat and grabs a key to open the house then tosses it back on the ground. We stomp up the stairs and directly into the kitchen where Irma pulls a bottle of tequila off the top of the refrigerator. She pours shots into coffee mugs. Mine says "World's Best Daddy." I bet that was a gift from one of her girlfriends. We throw the terrible liquid back quickly, do two apiece. I think it's two. It could have been three. But after we do them, I have that intense feeling of regret I've cultivated over the years. I immediately really wish I had not done shots, immediately. I wish I had stuck with my earlier affable drunk. Now my brain launches its betrayal. My thoughts spin a thousand miles per hour and it makes me feel completely unstable and kind of scared. I try to seem normal, which I guess is just for myself, since Irma would never judge me.

"I think I need to lie down," I say and guide myself along the counter toward Irma's bedroom. I transfer from one doorframe to the next and pitch toward the bed. My eyes fall closed immediately as a whiff of the patchouli-scented blanket wafts into my nose. I hear Irma say something about going to the Eagle for a drink but it's as though she's calling from tomorrow, too far away to hear clearly.

When I wake up again it's 6:32 a.m. and Irma is crawling under the sheets with me. She's naked except for her manundies and she slides up close to me. Her feet are freezing and she slides them up my calves so I push her away.

"Get those icebergs off me," I mumble and turn away from her. Next thing I know there is a hand creeping around my waist and to my belly. "Seriously Irm! What the hell are you doing?"

"I want to touch you."

"Hilarious. Sleep it off." She grumbles and turns over, then five seconds later, ripping-loud snoring. I start thinking about my brother anxiously. Worried he's going to fall apart again, worried this is going to jeopardize my new job, embarrassed that I'm just as worried about money as I am about him. Maybe it's a coping mechanism. Maybe I can't quantify the space he occupies in my life.

"Hey, dummy," my brother says as I roll up to Potrero del Sol to skate. He's leaning against the chain-link fence and drinking a beer. A small cooler sits on the ground next to him, his sweatshirt is bunched up on top of the cooler. His friend Matt sits on the ground next to the cooler eating handfuls of Lucky Charms cereal out of a box. They're high, I can feel it immediately. Matt has a big bandage on his dumb foot and it's stuffed in a Vans high top with the laces open to their limit. I don't even want to know.

"What up, fucker," I say, and skate off around the bowl. I drop in and roll out some lines, smooth sailing, a few mellow grinds. I pop out, skate around the perimeter, catch some air off that little hip/pointy thing next to the bowl. I roll back over to Peter for a beer.

"Gimme one of those."

"Okay, but then you have to drive us to Mendocino," he says, over-pronouncing "Mendocino" and staring directly into my eyes.

"When?"

"Today."

"I thought we were leaving tomorrow?" I ask. "And why can't we drive up separately?"

"Come on, don't be a bitch."

"It doesn't make me a bitch to . . ."

"Shut up, shut up!" he says in a singsong voice and rolls into the flow bowl. I wait for him at the cooler, drinking one of his beers. He rolls back up, breathing heavily.

"Rigo is having a birthday party in Ukiah tonight and I want to be there. He's been going to anger management classes and getting his shit together so I want to support him. Plus we work together now so I really need to be there for him."

"Why don't you take your own car?"

"Don't be stupid, you know my car can't keep doing that drive." He has this old brown Lincoln that is basically like if someone put a cardboard refrigerator box over a red wagon and drew doors on it.

"I know, but I need to be able to come and go as I please! I'm sorry, I don't want to check in with you anytime I go somewhere." I roll into the flow area and lay into a frontside grind on the extension that is so juicy it scares me. But somehow I stay on it and I'm fine. I love when that happens. I skate over to the bubbler for a drink of water and my brother sneaks up behind me.

"How about this. I'll pay for all the gas."

"I desperately need an oil change though."

"We'll do that first. We can stop at that place on Duboce and Valencia. Plus think about it, we can skate all the way up!"

"When do you want to leave?"

"Now?"

"Goddamn it. Fine. I'll run home to get my shit, and then I'll come get you."

"Already ready."

I start pushing out of the park and Peter yells after me, "I love you!" I laugh and wave. Two teenage dudes swing fists at each other half-jokingly just outside the skatepark fence and I'm not telling you that because it's a metaphor for me and my brother, it's just what I see.

Peter and I fly up the 101 toward Ukiah. It's an overcast day and cozy in my Forerunner. We have giant cups of coffee and I have a big bag of cinnamon gummy bears. Peter seems distracted. Even though we're off to do something fun he has a grim look on his face as he drives. I can sense something is bugging him. I have an eerie ability to know his mood better than he does. Maybe I'm kind of psychic.

I was going to say that once you're north of Santa Rosa, it feels like you're leaving civilization. But I think that's just reality, not a *feeling*. You go from a populated area to a less populated area. Boom. There are words for that. We push north and farmland opens up next to us, and deep valleys with water or just a bunch of rocks and burnt grass. I feel psychically unburdened getting into this part of California. Not so much relentless input and sensory overload. No one pooping in your doorway or fucking in the weird small space between your garage and front door. It's a beautiful, complex landscape, nature unfolding in satisfying, mathematical equations that your cells understand. Most signs of human existence are utterly bearable. A solar power vendor, an old general store, a ranch. Even gas stations seem less offensive up here. Well, barely. They're poops in the pool for sure but there's too much good up here to get undone about it.

We jump off the freeway to skate the old park in Healdsburg. Everything here is small but it's fun. The park is completely empty. Peter sullenly rolls off and I turn through the flow area, stretching my legs out and enjoying the cool, clean air on my face. There's a shallow bowl with metal coping that begins flush with the concrete then progressively sticks out more. I practice rolling in over the lower, easy part. I'm feeling giddy that I'm doing this without falling. After a couple times, through, I'm about to go again and Peter comes over.

"I saw you across the park and was like, 'Is she rolling in?' and I couldn't believe it. That's so rad, want me to film you?"

So we go to my starting point and push off with me in front and Peter behind me, taking video with his phone. I ride toward my entry spot but hit it diagonally, so my wheel gets hung up and I am pitched forward, then land on the concrete shoulder-first. Cruel pain shoots through my body, and I lie on the ground for a minute while I gather myself. Peter hovers above me.

"Holy fuck dude, are you okay? You get hung up?"

I stand up and get back on my board. I never leave a park right after an injury. That can't be the final note. I roll around, feel my shoulder pulse, and when I'm satisfied that I've stabilized, we get back on the road.

We continue up the 101. We pass a hippie school bus. But the people inside aren't in their sixties, they're more around twenty. A new and derivative generation! What do they feel strongly about? War? Sriracha? I don't know. But then I see this guy with long, curly, dark brown hair hanging out one of the narrow windows and I'm filled with love. He looks so sweet. His arms dangle down and his hair blows around his face while his eyes shine out. Is he as free as he looks? Does he ever feel terrible? There is an argument for realizing you never know what someone is going through or what their interior life is and so you back off with a big *who knows*, but then I can also conjure a great life in which I make huge assumptions about the lives of others and let it color my world. Rapturously conjuring crazy stories in my head is really no different than being addicted to *Days of Our Lives* except no commercial interruption in my mind, so, I win.

We blow past the bus and continue up the winding 101. Peter looks over at me. "Thanks for coming with me."

"I'm always down to party!"

"When you don't have a stick up your vagina."

"Oh my god *no*, you do not get to say that."

He gets a little smile. "There's some other stuff I need to do while I'm up here."

I wait for him to fill in the details. "Tell me what you mean!"

"I just have fucking stuff to do. Work. You'll need to entertain yourself sometimes. I might need to take the car and do stuff, so just figure out how you're going to handle your time."

"You can't just take my car! You take my car when I say it's okay!"

Peter jerks the wheel, hard. My head hits the window. I feel a gross echo through my skull, an ache. "Ow!" I yell. "What the fuck! Pull over right now. You can't drive anymore." I clutch my head and try to will the pain away. Peter slows the car and pulls to the shoulder, still rolling. "If I want to drive, I can! If I want to turn around right now, I can! You can't make me a prisoner in my own car. Stop and get the fuck out of the driver's seat."

Peter, after letting the car coast to show that he doesn't do anything just because I ask him to, finally stops and gets out. I want to punch him a thousand times and then kick him in the knees while they bleed and scoop his eyes out with a very sharp melon baller. This asshole brother of mine who was a little kid once and wore stupid outfits and had hair like a Lego man helmet. What a dummy. I climb over the middle console and get in the driver's seat. I am shaking with anger. My head aches. "I'm turning around," I say.

"Please don't."

"Why?" I look at him with what feels like the most concentrated vitriol.

"I can give you a chunk of money when we get to Ukiah. Well, probably more like tomorrow or the next day."

I stare at him, hard. I guess I'm trying to menace my way to some power here? "That's supposed to make up for being a hostile fuckface who just swerved and . . ."

"I'm sorry!" he yells like a frustrated, barking dog. "I'm fucking stressed out, can you let it go?"

I want to make him apologize more, and I want to feel like he really takes responsibility for the fact that he made me hit my head and I'm going to have a huge bruise. But I know that pressing the issue will just escalate things into more painful insanity so I decide to just be silent and get back on the road.

I drive north for a bit and try to calm down. Peter stays quiet and just stares out the window. I don't know why I'm not getting more remorse from him other than I never have and it's not his style. My stomach starts churning. It feels like shoes in the washing machine. Clogs. This happens to me sometimes from stress. I try to visualize lying on an empty beach on a tropical vacation but it keeps getting worse and I break into an intense sweat. I can feel I'm going to poop or barf or both immediately so I pull off at a gas station without saying a word. I get a key from a crusty old bearded guy and run to the bathroom. The second I get in there all hell breaks loose from my stomach. The pre-existing state of the toilet and surrounding area is not helping calm me at all. Crumpled-up toilet paper and indiscernible smears litter the floor. The garbage can overflows with detritus and the bowl itself has a ring of pointillist yellows and browns at the water level. After half an hour of heaving I'm sitting on the floor, which should really tell you something about how weakened and defeated I feel. My joints throb, maybe a disco beat. My head feels like the snow on an empty TV channel in a decade I never knew. When I hear someone pulling on the handle of the bathroom door shame overrules exhaustion and I drag my bones up and out to daylight. I bet I look like I was doing drugs. Or sleeping in a dumpster on a heap of rotten cabbage and wheelchair pieces. I choose not to even look at whoever is going in next. Poor slob.

When I get back to the car Peter looks at me with sorta sad donkey eyes. "Are you okay? That was a really long time."

"Thanks for checking on me."

"I thought you might want privacy."

"I don't know what you could have done anyway. I was just vomiting my brains out."

"You okay to drive?" he asks.

"I guess you probably should. Though I don't want you to. I swear if you do anything shitty I will cut the tips of all your fingers off."

Peter wordlessly takes over, and we travel the last for-ty-five minutes to Ukiah.

Peter and I roll up to the Redwood Inn, a small roadside motel painted all white with light blue trim. Cracked con-crete with sprouting weeds surrounds the low, sagging row of rooms. It looks like barracks for a grandma army. We've stayed here before, it's Pete's favorite spot. The Redwood Inn is owned by a couple of elderly drunks: two gay guys, Don and Phil. They can barely run the place and never pay attention to the guests, so it's perfect. That's probably part of why Peter stays here. Last time he was here was fucked. Which makes it feel a little strange to return. As far as I can tell, he had been clean for a few months and then got high and used too much. Fortunately before he got high he had texted Rigo who found him OD'ing in his motel room and took him to Ukiah Valley Hospital. Rigo said he had turned blue. He would have died if Rigo hadn't found him. The whole thing makes me so sick that my nerve endings ache. I drove up because Rigo texted me and told me what happened. Pete was pissed.

I felt embarrassed picking him up at the hospital after that. Hospital staff don't care about you when you OD. They have to save you but they do not like you, because you're taking their time from the injuries and maladies people supposedly didn't ask for. The nurses at Valley Med were efficient and just kind of cold when I came in. It made me feel very protective of my brother even though I was furious with him. When Pete was discharged he said "Thank you" to the nurse at the desk and the nurse said, "Why don't you get some real problems? We waste so much time and money with people like you, and I'm sure we'll see you again."

We both stared back at him, and I punched down every impulse in me to scream at the guy, because I wanted to get Peter home.

"Get some help. You have nice clothes, an iPhone in your pocket, your friend who brought you in, and whoever this is. We all have struggles," the guy went on.

"You don't know me," Pete said.

"I'm glad I don't. You're just a spoiled rich kid fucking up your life and you probably have a mother crying about you somewhere. Shame on you." He shook his head and looked down at his work. We turned around and left.

Yeah, our mom is crying about this and has for years. Seeing her try to pick a good strategy for dealing with Peter has been heart-wrenching. At this point she'll talk on the phone and give lots of love, but she doesn't send Peter money anymore, and she doesn't pay for lawyers when he gets in trouble.

We get our own rooms at the Redwood and Peter pays. It's better for us to have separate space if we don't want to end up on an episode of *20/20* as the siblings who successfully murdered each other at the exact same time. I want to achieve some kind of greatness in this lifetime but I'm really hoping it's not the kind that requires a criminal investigation.

Peter checks on me before going to Rigo's birthday party. I can't join. I'm happy to be alone owing to my hideous physical state. I throw up a paltry amount in the toilet, which is clean, fortunately. Then I endure spasming dry heaves for a few minutes. Every time I think of getting sick in the gas station bathroom earlier my body reacts with a wrenching lurch. My abdominal muscles are killing me and my throat is raw. Finally the heaves subside and I drag myself to the bed which stretches on forever, purple waves of grain, a generous California King. I peel my clothes off my aching skin and fall onto the cool sheets. I am a woman in her psychic Corvair, unsafe at any speed. I fall asleep lying on my side, with my stomach spilling beside me and whatever aches within it pulling down like a bag of rocks.

I wake up three hours later and glimpse dusk between the blackout curtains. Slowly I sit up, take a break, then walk to the sink area. It is completely, creepily static, electricity hum quiet. I stand before the long mirror completely naked. I look at myself and unexpectedly I like what I see. Like I snuck up on myself. I try to remember if I've ever felt this way before. I grab my toothbrush and clean my teeth then lie back down on the bed and turn on the television. I watch *Forensic Files* for a little bit then doze off. Sinister retellings of murdered women glow on me as I go in and out of consciousness in my hollow shell. I'm the rotting carcass of a noble animal. My organs have long since been eaten by wolves, consumed so quickly my body is still warm. The noble soldier nests in my eviscerated ribs, knowing what it means to make a sacrifice, and quietly thanking me for offering my remaining architecture as shelter.

I wake up in the middle of the night, an unborn hour heading for a sunrise abortion, and boldly decide to take a break from stories of women being murdered. I flip to some reruns. I tune in to a network show that is, zanily enough, about family. It begs the question: should rich people write TV? Because holy fuck these are without question the most boring people I've ever watched in my whole life. I swear this is why I watch so much *Dateline*. At least those murderous psychopaths have a story to tell.

I can't stop watching this show, called *Connecting* (sounds like a lesbian bar). I'm obsessed with how bland it is, and the unchecked flatness of the story they're telling. In this episode, *Stella is thinking of adding a cafe to her knitting store because her kid's getting older and will need money to pay for college. She hasn't been saving! But crap, she doesn't know how to make espresso drinks! She enrolls in a barista class. When she gets there, she's really overwhelmed by all the dudes with beards and ladies with brightly colored hair. She takes the class and darn it, in the end, she makes a very beautiful latte, despite what some would consider a lopsided heart in her foam design.* Why is this on television? I thought we were supposed to connect with these stories. Or was that just *Roseanne*? Is TV aspirational now, and does this mean our aspirations are to feel very little and have our conflicts be so mild that our constitutions become increasingly delicate and suited only to an aristocrat's existence? These are the questions of a privileged existence. Now I have myself all ramped up and it's 2:41 a.m. But there's nothing I have to wake up for so I give in to watching further machinations of the dull.

My brother wants me to go with him to the farm today. I admit I'm curious. Rigo picks us up in his dark green Datsun. We drive an hour or so to the scene, and I feel excited, like

I'm going to my own surprise birthday party knowing it's a surprise but I'm not supposed to know.

We walk up the path to the house, and I see a few tents scattered in the trees around us. Worker accommodations.

Rigo says, "Those are the ladies' tents."

"Where are the dudes?" I ask.

"We only hire women. Not to be creeps but because they're easier to work with. Men can get violent."

"For real," I say. "Do people get robbed?"

"I've heard of plenty individual trimmers and operations being robbed. Some scenes have a security crew with AKs protecting them. We don't have that as of now, but we're talking about getting a couple guys. I got some recommendations. There is a scene farther north about a hundred miles that has a lot of security. Huge dudes with AKs, surveillance cameras, locks, the works. The guys who run it are paranoid, very intense people. My friend Camille worked there. She said it was hell, that the stress wasn't worth the money."

My brother chimes in. "It's stupid to have a big farm. You make a shitload of money, but then you have to figure out where to hide it all. Whether to convert a bunch into gold before you bury it or if you want to bury a shitload of notes. At a certain point, you really aren't going to enjoy all that money."

"Anyway, a couple of their guards are leaving and looking for new work. So we could pick them up. Best to get people by word of mouth anyway."

We go inside. It's just a slightly crappy suburban house. We lived in one that looked a lot like it in Santa Rosa in the '90s. There are a couple of posters on the walls, an old sectional in the living room, and a giant round table in the middle. The table has a three-foot-tall skull bong sitting on it as though it was staged for a photo about *stoners*.

"Let's go back to my office, I have something for each of you," Rigo says.

We walk into his office, which has a rickety desk from the '80s and some plastic file bins on wheels. There's a mechanic's poster of a hot lady in a G-string and tiny boob covers next to his desk. Rigo reaches into a drawer and pulls out two little boxes, then hands one to each of us. Peter and I open our boxes at the same time, and inside of each is a *gold* vape. I'm beside myself.

"Fuck, dude. This is sick. Thank you so much," Peter says and fist-bumps Rigo.

"So dope!" I say.

"Paloma, your brother and I need a broker. We need someone who can sit down with individual customers and talk to them, show them everything we're producing and help them make choices. The broker needs to be good with these rich and famous types."

"Pete told me a little bit about it, I'm so down."

Rigo sets down a small stack of hundred-dollar bills. "Here's two thousand bucks. Like a signing bonus, except you're not Dwyane Wade, and I ain't the Bulls, so it's a little less."

"Holy Schlitz wow wow wow," I say, trying to think so fast about what to do.

"We good?"

"Yes," I say, as firmly and confidently as I can.

"Alright. Go check the plants with your brother and let him acquaint you with what you'll be selling."

We walk to the back of the house and enter a brightly lit greenhouse nested under heavy tree cover. "Hello, ladies," Peter says, walking down the aisles of plants, checking the soil and offering compliments. He tells me all sorts of stupid details I'll use to match people with the proper strains of cannabis. I feel rich already.

The next morning I wake up to a text from Peter saying he had to go "do some stuff" so I look to see if my car is still there and it is. But I decide to hang out next to the motel pool, read and nap. The pool is a small square job with a seven-foot deep end. Weirdly deep for such a small tub. There is a coarse rope with faded white and blue buoys bisecting the pool, and a super tall chain-link fence around the perimeter. Like I'm in a low-security luxury prison yard. I'm glad I don't have to go anywhere in case my guts revolt again.

At five in the afternoon, I get another text from my brother, and he asks if I want to meet him at a bar called The Dong Show. I arrive at The Dong Show, which is this pink building that looks like it used to be a Pizza Hut. When I walk in, there's a wood cutout of a hot dog dressed up as a dachshund waving at me, a pair of tongs in one paw and a beer in the other. It says, "What up, dog?" Inside there are low, rattan tables and chairs with plaid cushions scattered about. Posters of male models clad only in banana hammocks decorate the walls. They look like they are all from 1985. Lots of chest hair and mustaches. In each one the model has a cutout of a hotdog taped to one of their hands. If there were gay male fraternities (are there?), this would be their clubhouse. The crowd here seems mixed. No one flagship kind of person. I don't know if this is a gay bar or a wonderfully vital strain of camp.

It's 6:30 in the evening, which seems like a good hour for a drink. I order a greyhound from the bartender, a tall and hefty blonde gal wearing a visor. There's a food menu too, so I order a meal called The Sausage Party. It's two bratwursts on a bun with fries and cole slaw. I ask for no bun. I sit and sip my drink and then Peter walks in. I suck down my drink and stand up like a loosely-sewn-together stuffed elephant.

Peter hugs me. He holds me extra long and waits for me to hug him back but I just lean on him and sigh.

"Sister my sister!" He's boisterous. Every mood he has I ascribe to a drug. I try not to. I never succeed. Maybe this is coke? "What are you having?"

"I'll tell you what I'm NOT having, and that's a bunch of bullshit from you!" I say, trying to be funny. It's way too early, like maybe ten years early, to make this particular joke. I feel loud and inept. Like my vagina is hanging out of my jeans.

"Okay, jerk, I'm going to get us some drinks." Mood swing. He walks off. My face is hot and I focus really hard on not hating myself for sending things off the rails so quickly.

Peter sits back at the table with me and I can see he's jittery. His eyes dart around the room and he finishes his beer really fast. I can't tell what's going on, if it's excitement or anxiety. He looks at me.

"A guy I know is going to meet us here."

"Oh really? Do I know him?"

"No. A dude named Oscar."

"How do you know him?"

"We met a while ago. He supplied us with the starter plants for the farm. I recently bought a second load of plants from someone else, so this will either be awkward or he'll try to win our business back. Want to play pool?"

Two years ago my brother disappeared for six months. He told me he was "going to NorCal for a couple days," and then just didn't come home. My dad said he had been sent to jail, and he wasn't exactly sure why. That's how my family works: vague on details, big on emotion. Also, Peter tried to stab my dad like five years ago. I don't know if he was on drugs, wanting drugs, whatever state. I just know I was told about it a year after it happened and there was this dismissive exhaustion from my dad, like he thought I already knew, forgot he hadn't told me, and was already annoyed relaying the details. He told me with equal gravity that Peter flipped over his car while driving away, after my step-mom threatened to call the cops. Apparently *everyone was fine.* Then my dad bought him a new car. How does this in any way align with sanity?

I decide to say yes to playing pool with my brother. "Sure, but you know I'm horrible," I remind him.

"First, shots. Then, pool."

We drink our dumb shots of tequila and I realize I'm completely, unbelievably drunk. I guess I don't have much food in my stomach. I focus on closing the space between me and the pool table, then I spin my head around and around looking for the cues.

"You holding up alright there?" Peter asks.

"No problem," I say. "I'm sorry I said something stupid before."

"What are you talking about?"

"About not taking any bullshit, I was just trying to be funny and it wasn't."

"Oh. Whatever. I already forgot."

I chalk my cue with that purple powder which gets all over my fingers and somehow on my shirt. I try to brush it off but it smudges into the fabric. When I look in a beer mirror I see I have a big stripe on my left cheek. Peter breaks and we play and I'm definitely playing a little better than I do when I'm sober. At one point I think I've been lining up to shoot the solid blue number two ball for about ten years. I finally hit it, and when I look up my brother is talking to a big dude with black buzzed hair and a goatee.

"This is my sister, Paloma," Peter says. I give a huge, warm smile meant to make him adore me. "Paloma, this is Oscar." Oscar gives me a half smile and looks at me with eyes that are wary, so I try to remember if there is anything scary about me. He creeps me out but I push that feeling down quickly.

"You guys want to go to PJ's?" Oscar asks. "This place is like, too bright." I feel resistant to a change of venue. I was just getting relaxed. Plus now I wonder if Oscar is homophobic. I look at his eyes again. They are a rich chocolate brown with long black lashes. So pretty.

"Is Nancy working?" Peter asks.

"Yeah," Oscar responds and sadly, we leave The Dong Show.

We're in Oscar's car, which is an old Chevy Cavalier. Greyish blue. There is dog hair everywhere. I sit in the back and stare out the window, watching lights fly by and then just deep, country darkness. Stars. My feet are planted in a footwell sea of empty paper cups and plastic soda bottles.

We drive for what must be at least half an hour. I check in to the conversation in the front seat when I hear Peter say, "Where are you going?" and I realize that being in the country doesn't make sense with going to a bar. There are no lights, or stores, or houses.

"Going to get gas at that cheap place out here."

"Really?" Peter asks.

"Yeah, it's a dollar less per gallon than the places in town," he says and chuckles to himself. I want to say something that makes everything normal but I'm scared. I can't figure out a logical reaction because the feeling of drunkness keeps washing over me.

We come up to a gas station and Oscar pulls off the road.

There is a low cement wall that is painted with an ocean scene, a big dolphin at the center. Oscar rolls up to a gas pump and does not turn off the car. He looks straight ahead and says, "How much money do you have?"

"I don't know," Peter says and meets Oscar's gaze.

"Give me your fucking wallet. And your phone." Oscar is utterly impassive.

Pete doesn't do anything but stare at Oscar.

"Don't make this fucking ugly, dude. Don't make me do something that's going to suck in front of your sister. Give me your goddamn wallet and phone."

Peter pulls out the beat-up leather wallet my dad gave him for Christmas years ago and throws it into Oscar's lap. Oscar opens it up and looks at the bills. Peter reluctantly hands over his phone too.

"Forty-three dollars, huh? You're rich. Here, go get me a Twix." Oscar throws two dollars at my brother. Peter opens his door and gets out of the car so I do too. I walk next to him and we go into the mini mart and sure enough, we hear Oscar drive away.

"Dude," Peter says, with deep seriousness. I don't say anything because I'm experiencing an internal refusal to connect with reality. "We're screwed," he says and a long smile stretches across his face. "That's a fucking long walk. Do you have your phone?"

I check and find that I left my phone at the motel. We both start laughing and then we can't stop. Everything seems hilarious. Being abandoned, the bright lights, the rows of candy, the beef jerky. The lighters and the antifreeze. The half-obscured issues of *Jugs*. By the time we pay, we both have tears rolling down our cheeks from laughter.

We buy a lot of candy with my money. My pockets are

lumpy and misshapen with crappy chocolate and when we step out into the night it is just us and a walk to town.

"Why exactly did we get ditched?"

"Well, guess he chose the anger option over the getting-our-business-back option."

We walk along the road, two lanes of asphalt and no lights. The shadows are dark and wet off to the side, surrounded by trees, and light from a half moon falls on the road in front of us. I link arms with Peter and we walk that way for a long time, taking in the darkness and merging with the silence.

"Pete?"

"Jah."

"Should I be worried that you're not, like, sober anymore?"

He's quiet for a moment. "I got this. Don't worry about me."

"Okay," I say, even though I strongly suspect it is not.

We walk for an hour and a half I'm guessing and we see a bright sign ahead. It says "LIQUOR." I have exactly fourteen dollars left so we have to make this count. We pick out a couple of Pabst tall boys and I pay the dude at the counter.

"How far are we from town?" Peter asks.

"Which one?" the guy asks.

"Ukiah."

"Oh, about sixteen miles."

"Fuck," I burp involuntarily. I kinda hope it will make the guy smile but he is impervious to my body's jokes.

A guy behind us in line, maybe twenty-five years old with a backwards baseball hat, asks, "You having car trouble?"

"We're walking and it is way further than we thought," I say.

"I can take you to town if you want. Promise I won't kill you!" Fortunately, he has the right audience for this dark joke.

We ride with this guy, whose name is Terrence, into town. It is such a relief to have the help I could cry, but instead I drink my tall boy in the back seat and watch the darkness pulse outside.

Peter and I finally arrive at our motel. The parking lot in front of my room is dark, and the pavement is wet. When I reach into my pocket for my key it's just not there, which is no surprise. I walk over to the office to see if I can get another. The glass door is propped open and when I walk in there's an old guy with white hair and beard and mustache pacing the room and smoking. He wears glasses with thin metal frames. A serial killer vibe, like so many white guys. From the smell of things, I gather he's been lighting one cigarette off the other for hours, maybe his whole life. The lobby is various shades of taupe. There is a dusty basket of fake flowers on the counter next to a bell. A large painting of a little girl walking a Schnauzer down a cobblestone street is on the wall. I like imagining them picking it out at a flea market.

"Hey, I lost the key to my room, can I get another?" Without a word he hands another key over. I grab it and run out like I robbed him. I pretend he's chasing me, all the way back to my room. Peter stands waiting for me.

"Weirdo," he says.

When we're inside Peter cracks open two beers for each of us. I start pulling my pants down on the way to the bathroom and walk in with my jeans around my ankles, underwear sagging on my butt, and leave the door open while I pee for what seems like ten minutes.

"Hold my calls!" I yell then sip my beer. In at the top, out at the bottom. I lay my head on my knees and wait. I look at the little tiles on the floor. I see the shape of a lion's head. I see a dumb daisy. A UFO. A cake stand.

When I walk out, Peter hands me another beer even though the two I have aren't finished. "Let's go swim in that pool," he says.

The pool fence is locked with a big chain, so we start climbing over it, each of us holding three beers. I'm really proud of our gusto. I tuck two of my cans in the back of my jeans, one in each pocket. Good thing I'm wearing the hugest pair of crappy corduroys known to man. As I climb the open beer sloshes onto the butt of my jeans and soaks all the way through to my skin. The cool air grazes my warm face softly, like a liquid. A liquid, soft, lady hand. A long lady model hand slathered in Jean Naté or Love's Baby Soft. The night sky is full of stars, visible even over the bright light of the motel sign.

By the side of the pool Peter and I strip down to our underwear. We enter the water carefully, using the stairs, so we can swim with our beer. I drift around the pool blissfully. I use one hand to paw at the warm water and I hold the other in the air to keep my drink aloft, a sloppy sidestroke. I love the bluish light on my brother's face. His is such a complicated heartache. I love the quiet. If I don't concentrate or clamp down on my brain for any reason I can feel like right now is beautiful and perfect.

One thing that I do but don't want to do is heavily psychoanalyze about how Peter ended up this sad (angry?) donkey drug addict. There were plenty of betrayals from our young parents and there was violence in the house and all that stuff you hear people pointing to when they are trying to describe why they are a certain way. Picking someone apart is a stupid distraction and I'm not sure Freudian psychology has all the answers. Why does the effort to understand each other somehow preclude an acceptance of complexity? How can you be shitty and great at one time? How can you love me and still steal my money? Alright, I'm done, I already feel gross trying to articulate this stuff.

After two beers I start to feel faint and weird. My mind goes fuzzy and I let myself drop down to the bottom of the pool, sinking and sinking while water fills my mouth. I feel so weightless that I become disoriented and I can't get to the surface. I keep reaching and trying to maneuver but nothing feels right. The noiselessness of water swaddles me. I dated a girl, very crazy, who said she always wished she was a shark because it's so peaceful under water. What was the mental soundtrack to her waking life? I imagine non-stop subway brakes in her ears. As I sink everywhere I look I see the same shade of blue. A jet. Air sky wall chlorine California dream down to sleep at night. I let go and wait for the bottom to catch me. There is a tunnel of relief, feeling the bottom catch you.

Suddenly I am pulled up by my shirt and Peter drags me to the side of the pool. I grab on to the concrete edge and gasp while I wait for my head to clear. Peter watches me wordlessly and drinks his beer. My face hurts from coughing. Big repulsive veins in my face are all I feel, with a tree trunk of snake belly throat.

"Don't do that," Peter says. "Don't drown."

Eventually our teeth chatter and we go back to our respective rooms for hot showers. It takes superhuman strength to remove my clothes and get in the shower. My body. I feel like a pair of nylons filled with old shoes.

I try not to look at myself in the mirror usually. Which is probably sad or not self-loving somehow. If I look I'll start picking myself apart and finding things to feel bad about so it's easier not to start.

When I climb into my bed with my hot skin I run my feet all over the cool, coarse cotton and it feels so good. My head spins. I turn on the TV where there are more *Forensic Files*. I guess as long as women are being murdered by their boyfriends they will keep making shows. I watch for a few minutes, then roll over on my face and drop out. I sleep deep drunk sleep until five in the morning when I wake up and can't fall back in. I try but can't because the booze has worn off and nausea and shame churn in my guts. I'm naked.

I put on an enormous pair of sweatpants and an old sweatshirt of Peter's. I step outside and sit in a white plastic chair outside my door. The air is thick with fog and cold. For a second there is not another living soul but then a lady rolls by on a ten-speed bicycle. She is in a tube top and tiny jean shorts. How is she not freezing? She rides with one hand on the handlebars and her other hand holds a shotgun, just casual at her side, pointing at the ground. She looks at me for one second and continues. I know it sounds like I'm making this up just to be funny but it's real.

I stare at the wet road and redwood trees towering on the other side. I drift to my Mediocre Comedian fantasy.

I get onstage. Tank top. A haircut you just didn't expect on a woman! What! The ultimate white lady incursion, far beyond gay: a non-traditional hairstyle! What would embolden a woman to flout convention so carelessly? Has she no care for the opinions of others? Hath she not abundantly reaped the approval of her caretakers and peers such that long hair (with cute layers) is not her default? This one went off the rails.

Good evening, everyone! I am a woman comedienne! Impossible, you say? I'm not interested in the limitations of your understanding!

Allow me to start with an apology: I'm sorry. As a woman, I know that can grease the wheels of your tolerance for my existence. I will work in some pratfalls and try to fall in love while we're here so that additional opportunities to feel favorably toward me materialize, thus allowing my performance to propel my career through another day mopping the decks of this ten-story luxury cruise ship called life.

Have you ever noticed that skirts make your legs feel close together? Sometimes my left leg is so close to my right that I can hear it breathing. Frankly, I prefer the double-privacy curtain of pants. My right leg wants to doze on its ventilator and emit trumpet farts without the left leg noticing.

I am a strong woman.

If I stare at a pillowcase long enough, I can see it undulate.

If I wash dishes all day every day, nothing meaningful happens (thankfully).

When I spend the proper chunk of money, my hair grows thicker and my eyelashes graze my forehead.

When I want to help raise other people's children, I am underpaid. When I request a respectful wage, friends I care about look down on me. It is an honor to be considered at all.

Have you ever noticed that the heavier your period gets, the more your body wishes it was a wind turbine? A giant, smooth, cool metal generator of energy, never a California condor caught in its heavy and dutiful blades.

Can you imagine what it would be like to wake up feeling like you own the whole country every day? Me neither. I can imagine what it feels like to wake up and know I own three cats though, and I suspect that feeling goes better with my figure, which goes in at the middle and flares at the hips into what my mother calls "a pear shape." Sometimes I look down at my underwear and the uninterrupted smoothness from my belly to my anus and I think, "No dick there." It's such a curiosity, what goes on in your underwear. And mine!

Being a woman entitles you to an embarrassment of tiny shoes. We all know about the wage disparity stuff and rape and eating disorders. Let's get into the spoils. Waistbands that create lifelong dents above your navel that are best displayed in the locker rooms of gyms where you try like hell to battle small evolutionary necessities like hormones and stress, the cultivation of creative postures that make walking with pencils under your heels look "natural," access to empathy that makes being alive and seeing what sick fucks roam this earth unbearable on a minute-to-minute basis, and let us not forget: a passion for shell art! A frog made of tiny shells: this is living! Whimsy meets vulnerable, for sale at a gas station.

I don't want to part with a sentiment that gives the impression that my eyes are closed to the reeking pile of bullshit we face every day. Or that the delicate head on my big feathered body is buried in so much sand, I mean discarded tires.

I like to say that a fart was the first joke our Creator made, and that women were the second. And what an excellent comic that clown is, because look: we're all still laughing at both.

Today is my first day of work on the mountain. I bought a tent and I guess I'm just going to stay on the land while I work? It's really beautiful here. Lush hills, crazy tall redwoods, and everything always feels damp. I came to work with my hair still drying from my shower at the motel, and I have a feeling it's never going to fully dry.

The scene is basically a two-story rundown house and the trimmers are in a long room with two big rectangular party tables set up end to end. A few people have ear buds and iPods. I'm not listening to anything besides the quick clipping sounds in the room. Some people are chatting. I'm watching just to see how everything goes. I need to get intimate with our operation and our product. I guess it does make me a little nervous that technically I'm sitting in an illegal operation. Going to jail is a big fear of mine. So is being trapped in a narrow space with rats. I know there are raids up here sometimes. Helicopters fly around to help law enforcement find farms. But the fact is, I believe that people should have access to marijuana. I think it can be used healthfully. I would feel very different about trafficking heroin, or meth, or crack, or anything like that. Those are the evil drugs that can't be used recreationally. Even though weed is set to be legal in California, there are enough technically illegal demands for product that pay a high premium and are worth the risk. It doesn't feel any worse than trespassing to skate a pool.

I sit on a stool like the ones in an art class, a squat little grey one with a round disk of particleboard for a seat. I try to keep my spine straight. That lasts for about three minutes. My brother gave me a pair of very sharp and tiny scissors, like he was a jeweler displaying a diamond necklace. I use them to trim intricate little waves through stalk after stalk of cannabis. I drop the trimmed bits into a plastic tub. It is mind-numbingly boring work. I try to just focus on the money I'm earning. Technically it seems like I should be able to make this meditative. But I don't want to meditate for twelve hours.

My butt starts killing me so I go upstairs to say hi to Peter. The interior of the house is pretty boring. Just white walls with that texture stuff. A couple framed posters that seem like they were bought at a thrift store just to make the place feel normal, if normal is a freshman dorm. There is a cross-stitched piece with three owls sitting on a branch, and a fourth owl hanging upside down on the branch. It says, "Why Be Normal?"

I knock on Peter's office. It's funny to have an office at a weed farm. I get why it makes sense, but also I thought they would fuck with the configuration a little more. It feels like he could be working at a paper company or something. I tap on the door. It's hollow. With a modest amount of pressure I think my fist would go right through it.

"What?" he yells.

"It's me!"

"Who's 'me'?"

"Your sister, dum dum!"

"Come in, but close the door behind you."

I open the door and see Peter standing behind his desk with a semiautomatic gun. At least that's the name for it that runs through my head, though I don't know what exactly that means. It's all taken apart and he's cleaning it. I get a deep chill that hurts between my eyes.

"What do you want?"

"I needed to take a break, my butt . . ."

"You think you know it all already?"

"Yes, and I came up here to tell you how good it feels."

"Can't really trim much if you're up here bugging me." Peter is cleaning his gun the whole time he speaks to me. He glances up quickly only once or twice. Why does he even know how to clean that insane gun? Why would someone in my family know that? I've seen guns like this on TV, but I never saw one even once in my house growing up. I guess I saw rifles. I had a friend who took me to shoot clay pigeons one time in junior high. I can't even remember if I hit one, so I guess I probably didn't. I absolutely would have felt victorious. Her family was big into guns.

"But this isn't my real job anyway. I'm just getting to know the buds, so why does it really matter if I trim fast? Why don't you tell me about my first client so I can get my presentation together?"

"I actually just got the details," he says. "You're going to Los Angeles next week."

"What! Fuck yes! I can skate pools on my way down, party zone USA! So who is my client? Miley Cyrus? Gillian Anderson. Lisa Ling!"

"Go downstairs and work, and Rigo will come down to tell you what you need to know for your trip."

"Come on, you're not going to tell me?

"Rigo has all the information."

"You must know though."

"Go work."

"Sometimes you are the least fun person I've ever met."
I go back downstairs and sit down to work. I introduce myself to the lady sitting next to me. She's named Carlotta. She is trimming and chatting with a hippie lady named Soleil. She's a white lady with dreadlocks knotted on top of her head. She's not even wearing gloves or a mask, total novice move that young people make trying to Look Cool. Breathing in all the crystals off the plants can mess you up and give you a terrible cough, plus your fingers get super sticky and itchy. She has a sexy hippie outfit, a gross mishmash of brown cotton triangles crudely sewn together into a low-cut tank dress with no bra. She's barefoot. She can wear whatever the fuck she wants of course but it's not my job to deny it's a stupid outfit. I look down at my dumpy large T-shirt with a couple

Tom of Finland dudes on it, sporting their huge dongs and cop fetish wear. Below that I have some voluminous corduroy cut-offs and slip-on Vans that are a little long in the tooth. The perfect outfit for a lady. I sit at the end of the table and work on my own bag of buds, listening to those two talk. Carlotta tells Soleil how genetically modified food is bad for you. Soleil counters that she's been vegan her whole life and she only eats what comes out of the ground.

"Hey Soleil," I say, kinda loud. She looks at me with a sweet face, Carlotta slightly less so. "Where did you grow up?"

"San Francisco," she says.

"Really? What neighborhood?" I ask, purely to be a dick, a gamble that she's actually not from the city and therefore a suburban idiot which I somehow have the right to shit on.

"Well I was born in the Panhandle but we moved to Walnut Creek when I was like ten months old," she says.

"Not really from the city," I say.

"I spent a lot of time there," she says.

"My point remains the same," I say, and cool it, now I've shot all the fish in my personal dick barrel.

"What kind of name is Paloma?" she asks.

"It means 'dove' in Spanish."

"Are your parents from some, like, Spanish-speaking country?"

"Nope. My mom speaks Spanish but doesn't have any of that heritage. My parents were just stoners. Hippies trying to make me into a certain kind of person," I say and try to smile, fatiguing of my asshole routine.

"Cool. My dad says my great-grandmother was Miwok."

"Sometimes I think the whitest thing a person can do is claim a trace amount of Native blood that they know nothing about," I say, back in the game.

"Seems a little whiter to ignore genocide and think anything less than being a full-blood and living on the rez is negligible," Soleil says, suddenly stepping to me and entirely catching me off guard. I stop speaking and trim.

One month later, I haul ass in my truck down Highway 99. My chest is a little buzzy with anticipation. How will it be to meet with these people in L.A.? The pothead celebrities. One is an older rapper guy and the other is a young pop star lady. What if they're weird? What if they're mean? What if I fuck up and say things I'm not supposed to or insult them somehow? What if I don't know how to act and it's weird and obvious that I'm new at this and utterly unable to be normal?

I pull off the freeway to hit this backyard spot that a friend of Peter's named Scum has in a small town called Pixley. He said the guy is a little spesh, so my guess is that means he's a methhead or something. Hopefully he's ugly and nice at least. I park in front of a run-down generic suburban home with a completely dead lawn and a cracked sidewalk up to the front door. There's this weird little concrete pond next to the front porch but super tiny, like a foot across. There's a crappy plastic baby doll sitting in it. No clothes on it, no more hair, just naked and dirty. A disrespected college art major feminist baby. There are a couple random kids' toys scattered about: a blue plastic shovel, a deflated rubber ball next to a beer bottle with no label. There's a plastic sunflower on a metal pole stuck in the ground. It's super faded, and there's no wind to make it spin. I knock on the door and no one answers. The curtains are closed. I can't tell if anyone is there, though Peter said he is absolutely always there.

I walk around the side of the house. There's a cruddy

cinder block wall around the backyard. I pull myself up and look over. I see the bowl Pete told me about. I'm not sure if there are dogs. I don't want to deal with dogs. I don't have it in me to run. I jump down and go back to the front. The door looks slightly ajar, so I wonder if he looked out. I go back up and knock again. The door drifts open. The inside is dark and it smells intensely moldy. Like a leaky pipe has been festering under a kitchen sink or something. Kinda putrid. I swallow my doubts and walk in. There's a very weathered baby blue sectional, a coffee table, and little else in the room. Nothing on the walls, which were certainly white at some point, but now have a dirty, cobweb-y surface mottled with that cottage-cheese-like texture. A giant broken ashtray sits on the table. Where it's cracked, the ashes pile on the table. A guy appears in the doorway and his shorts are twisted at the waist. He doesn't seem to notice. Does that hurt your dick? Maybe he can't feel anything. Some people can't. There are a lot of reasons that might be true, like your nerve endings are deadened by leprosy or your brain doesn't work properly. His shirt is for someone about two feet shorter than he is. Like what are you, a British mod rocker from the '70s? Where's the bowl cut and puppy dog eyes? This guy's eyes are flat, over-cooked pancakes. His hair is thin, fried tufts. He's wearing high-top Vans with no socks. I could enjoy the visual hilarity of him if I wasn't a little scared about being caught walking around in his house with no permission.

"What up, are you Paloma?"

"Yeah, did my brother tell you I was coming?"

"Yeah, the fucker sure did. Want a beer?"

"Sure."

"There's some in the fridge. Grab one, I'll meet you outside."

I walk through to the kitchen and crack the refrigerator. A toxic fart cloud exhales out at me when I open the door. I suspect the lone take-out container on the top shelf is the culprit. There is a cardboard box of PBR cans open on the bottom shelf. I reach in and grab one. There is a nearly empty bottle of orange juice and a jumbo Kit Kat bar. I let myself out a sliding glass door to the backyard. There's a peanut-shaped bowl, so I drop in and take some runs. A guy who is not the first guy hobbles out of Scum's house on crutches. He has little saddle bags on each of his crutches and I see a beer peeking out of one of them. He's got a cigarette hanging out of his mouth and maybe not a full set of teeth. He has a navy blue cast from his toes to over his knee. I never ask the specifics on injuries because I don't want to visualize it for myself.

"Hey man," I say, and walk over. "Want me to grab a chair for you?"

"Sure, just fuckin' . . . I don't know, wherever," he says. I grab a white plastic chair and set it up near the bowl.

"I'm Paloma."

"John. Sorry, I'm pretty fucked up right now, wasted, it's not . . . whatever, you get it. . . ."

"You don't have to be sorry. How about I'm sorry your leg is a mess and you can't skate?"

"Yeah it's pretty jacked, I . . ."

"It's cool, I don't need to know."

"Right on."

"Is Scum putting his face on or something? He's gonna skate, right?'

"Yeah he just likes to do some things beforehand." John says, his eyeballs skittering around.

"It looks like it's gonna rain," I say, looking at the grey mashed potatoes above us. I pull my own chair over. The seat is dusted with a thin layer of dirt. I run my hand over it and the schmutz just sticks to my fingers, but doesn't otherwise brush off. It's greasier than it looked. I crack open my beer and look at my feet. They're small. I think I'm going to regret being here. I can kind of feel it. Nothing physically harmful is going to happen. But these people feel bad to me. It feels like drugs. I meet guys sometimes and all I can think is they've smoked crack and had sex with a wasted woman through a hole in her nylons the same night. It's too much sad shit. The hole in the nylons thing—I know that can happen between consenting adults who are not psychically spiraling down-ward. I let my friend Joni fuck me while I was wearing a vintage swimsuit one time, just by pulling the crotch panel over, okay? It's not that I'm being a judgmental asshole. It's just that about seven years ago I was sitting in a cafe and this ultra-gross dude was sitting next to me with his friend and talking about having sex with a lady through a hole in her nylons in a van while smoking crack and that was before he went to prison and got sober. So I can only be repulsed when I think of fucking through nylons. Sorry.

I skate for a little bit and mostly feel out of place, like I've stepped away from my fate on this earth and am in a weird rip in the space/time continuum. It's so baffling to be around people I can't connect with at all. I get back on the road. I try to drive a while with nothing on the radio. Now I'm listening to Barbra Streisand. I only have a *Greatest Hits* album but it's so good. I can see the grapevine ahead of me. There are still a lot of storm clouds gathered, but no rain yet. I see a little blue ahead, and it feels very disappointing. I want it to rain. I want to feel knit into an ennui bodysuit. I'm not ready for sun. I understand how grossly metaphorical that all sounds, and maybe by coincidence it *is* a metaphor, but I mean it literally. I feel betrayed by the return of the sun when the promise of rain hasn't been delivered.

My hotel, the Mü, is nuts. You walk in and the entry room is like the library of a trophy hunter. Wait, no, oh my god, those are the worst people. Like someone who is very rich and also an outdoorsman. There are geodes on the shelves! There is a basket with glass balls, some thick volumes of literature, canonical man shit like *War and Peace*. There are little ship sculptures and more ephemera that's random but still cohesive and classy. The shelves are wood. The couches are leather. There's a clear glass pitcher of water with cucumbers and lemons in it, and tumblers next to that. Not even plastic cups. This joint must cost thousands per night, not even for the fanciest rooms. Rigo had the people who are bringing me here book the room. I am on the west side of Los Angeles, apparently. Everyone I've run into looks fancy. I feel self-conscious about my finger tattoos.

My room is vast, and I have two queen beds. There's a separate room with a lounge area and TV. What if I spent every last dime I had staying here and then the day I left, I had no plan of what to do with the rest of my life? That would be dark. I bet some people do it. They don't let themselves think about the giant anvil hanging over their heads.

I'm seeing the lady tonight and the guy tomorrow. I unzip my big wheelie bag and take out all my samples. I bought pretty aqua blue Ball jars to hold the buds, and then these other vintage Pyrex containers for the edibles. It looks beautiful. I have a batik cloth and some candles, though I'm concerned the candles push it over into feeling contrived, like I'm an Avon lady. But I do think most people like a show, and a world to immerse themselves in. So I light the damn candles.

I receive a text that Embers is on her way to my room. I've been instructed not to ask anything about her personal or professional life unless she brings it up. I faxed a signed NDA to her lawyer. Honestly, what do I care about this 25-year-old folk musician? It's a little self-important of them to think I even know who she is much less am dying to Barbara Walters her face off. How about *my* rider says she can't ask about me? What if I simply find it intolerable to be questioned by an ambitious musician? I never agreed to think anyone was better than me just because they're famous and frankly, I resent having any conversation predicated on that idea.

There is a single, firm knock at my door. I get up and pull it open just a crack, like I'm not sure who is there. Upon seeing an enormous bodyguard whose physical person is like a pickup truck turned on end, I open the door wider.

"Good evening, sir," I say, with a deferential bowing of my chin, closing my eyes. "Welcome." He enters alone, and takes a couple minutes to inspect my space. Then he gets the lady, who arrives with another bodyguard, equally huge, though differently distributed in the realm of body mass. If the first guy is a pickup truck on its end, this guy is more an anaconda digesting a hippo. His head is little, bald, and pointed, and he is quite wide through the middle. Embers is beside him, a study in the disease that is charisma. She absolutely shines. You would have to be made of cigarette butts and Styrofoam to ignore her draw. Her soft lips reflexively part into a large smile, and her eyes dance. This is some Kennedy-level chemical manipulation. She's wearing a cream-colored peasant blouse, suede shorts and matching booties. Why would you wear anything but sweatpants when you're not performing or going out for dinner? Sweatpants are the only real way for your body to be free. Otherwise there's a seam up your vagina, a wrinkle is digging into your armpit, your boob is hanging out at a horrible angle or grotesquely emphasized by a distortion, making you look pornographically available when you don't want to be. To avoid all of *that* you have to yank and pull and arrange your dumb outfit every minute. Which no one can honestly say they want to do. I guess the overall comforts of being rich could make minor inconveniences like an ill-fitting shirt or pants drifting north less of a bother. Who knows what those people think, beyond "I better marry someone of my class," and "My siblings and I all went to prestigious universities and are now doing Important Work." Do I think there are rich people who live without a hole inside themselves? Probability tells me there must be, but popular evidence begs to differ.

"I brought you a little gift bag," Embers says, handing me a shiny black bag.

"Oh wow you didn't need to do that!" I sputter.

"Don't worry about it, girl," she says, and starts looking around my display on the table. She pulls off lids, inhales, murmurs approvingly. I dig through my gift bag and there are little soaps, a jar of face cream, a bottle of perfume, and a gift certificate to a massage place. Which pretty much cements that I'll come down here anytime she wants me to.

I take a deep breath and launch into my spiel. "Okay, so I have a range of products here that can do things like treat anxiety, help you sleep, make your mind sharp, make you . . ." I pause, because I loathe the word "horny" but can't think of any other word that has that meaning. "Make you, like, wanna screw. I have salves for aching muscles, and some stuff that's really good for period cramps. I have tampons that are soaked in CBD that really make your cramps go away."

She picks up every little jar and I give her samples of

several kinds. The names of these strains are generally predictable hippie riffs: Ben and Gary, Wavy Lady, Purple Phase, Nutri-Brain.

Do I think this lady is cute? I do. But I can't decide if it carries a sexual note to it. Like sometimes I just want to have sex with a lady and I think it's an animal thing more than a monogamous love thing. It just seems fun to roll around with a woman who is kind of like me in the gender way, a couple of broomsticks with wigs on them tumbling around in bed. Why do people have sex anyway? I feel my body want it but my mind is not strongly pulled in any way beyond what feels like curiosity. What will it be like to be naked next to this person? Will we make fun of anything? Will we like the same stuff? What gross moles does she have? What is her vagina doing? Will I go in thinking I'm casual and then be so in love I can't get my life together without this woman I thought I was only boning?

I went to my friend Steve's wedding a few years ago. He's from Texas. I wore a cute sundress, or kind of cute, it looked like it was made out of someone's bold curtain choice, I guess like in *Sound of Music*. The dress was black and white. I walked into the bathroom, and lots of blonde Texan ladies were gathered around the mirror fixing their makeup. I walked in and they looked at me and then one of them exclaimed, "Oh my god, you're so pretty!" and I won't deny that it made me feel good. Then I had a bunch of ladies around me just fawning and being sweet in an utterly confusing but deeply enjoyable way. I wanted us all to have sex. To get in bed with our hair and our legs and fuck each other, bat boobs and giggle. I was surprised for this to become one of my sexual fantasies. Before this moment I would have considered that some shallow bullshit but now I understand it is shallow perfection. I had a girlfriend at that time and she loved bringing up the Texas cheerleaders (I don't know if they were actually cheerleaders but I took that erotic liberty) to get me going. It really worked. It made me uncomfortable to be honest about liking those ladies. It just felt so *normal*. So expected. Can't I have a thing about a bunch of Wiccan bitches? No. Deep down I'm just a basic idiot.

Embers buys a jar of muscle salve, a bunch of sativa hybrid gummies and two ounces of four different kinds of weed I'm carrying.

"I entertain sometimes," she says.

"Cool," I say.

I text my brother in code to let him know what I sold.

"Holy fuck dude, you're killing," he writes back. I'm happy. I eat a brownie and watch episodes of *48 Hours* in bed until I fall asleep.

The next night I feel really confident that I'll do well again. I'm sitting on the weird couch with my display laid out. I text my brother that I'm going to try and top last night's sell. This seems like such a strong bonding point for us: excelling at the art of drugs. I look forward to us having this drive in common, since every other connection I thought was obvious has been a bust (blood, same alcoholics raising us, etc.) He writes back, "Second day in detox."

I write, "What?"

"Detox."

I don't know what to say.

"Don't freak out."

"OKAY I WON'T, THANKS BRO, SUPER MELLOW DETOX ZONE NORMAL THING FOR HEALTHY PEOPLE TO DO."

"Good. I'm out in a week. I'll text you."

"Can't wait. Does detox mean you'll be less of a cranky fuck or is that just your cool personality?"

"Don't fucking come at me right now."

"When is better? Do I ever get to tell you how fucking hard and weird and sad it is to want to know if my shithead brother is healthy or safe when he doesn't want to tell me and treats me like dripping diarrhea in a human suit?"

He doesn't write back to me after that. I feel sorta buzzy in my body, tense in my neck. If he's going to rehab that means something bad happened. I want to know what it was and I really don't want the pain of knowing. I can't win in this scenario.

I pull out a small bottle of whiskey and pour myself a glass. A couple burning sips and a warm feeling comes over me.

Sometimes I just want to bog down and ache for my weaknesses, feel profoundly sad and impenetrable to the mundane details of life because the shitty feeling is unimpeachable, it is defining, and I've given myself to it. But then I think I just like the feeling of being untouchable and I never end up getting anything out of feeling like shit for a stretch besides more of that stockpiled anger and misanthropy that makes me want to duck out of this shithole life sooner rather than later.

Just as I'm losing myself in mopey feelings there's a knock on my door, and I see the rapper dude, Gil, is here. He rolls in five deep.

"Hey baby!" Gil says warmly, arms open to embrace me. His eyes let me know he's already stoned as fuck, and maybe he has been for years now. He hugs me warmly; it feels good.

"Hey, I'm Paloma," I say.

"Gil. These are my boys." He indicates the men around him, and they all give a sorta contained "What up?"

"Come sit on my weird couch. Do you want anything to drink?" They all demur, and we sit down. They're immediately absorbed in my product, so I answer lots of questions and put together a package for them.

"You coming back down here anytime soon?" Gil asks.

"I can come down anytime."

"I'm gonna send you a couple colleagues."

"Just set it all up with Rigo and I'll be here."

"Right on."

I feel the room relax. We end up getting high for hours, slumped in the furniture and talking shit about every dumb thing in the world. At a certain point they leave, and when I get in bed I see it's 1:30 in the morning. I sold a lot to those guys. I'm going to let myself sleep in tomorrow and not even feel anxious about it.

I'm driving north on Highway 5, the most boring and occasionally offensive livestock-stench, glaring-sun freeway California has to offer. It's flat and straight and ugly. Who are all these drivers and where are they going? Will anyone ever launch a major publicly funded campaign to promote the rules of the road? Slow cars to the right. Passing lane to the left. It's simple but it gets disrespected constantly. Driving emphasizes that America is full of people with no sense of civic responsibility. There are millions of people using the freeway system, only a handful of whom are invested in making it flow for everyone.

I feel very good about the work I did in Los Angeles. Rigo is going to be stoked. I don't know that he's the best dude in the world but I would rather not police that. It's exhausting.

We all leak bile, psychic and otherwise. We all are vulnerable to wounds that can open up and expel spider babies. I don't think compassion for the actively abject is easily accessed by the average human. Can we not see each other's hearts and then say, "I value you"? According to mass shootings and city grocery cart recon trucks, I think not. With a nod to rape kits going unprocessed for decades. I coasted down a freeway off-ramp recently and saw a slim human yank their pants down and poop with extraordinary gusto all over the sidewalk. It grossed me out and made me feel happy that there are still behaviors that can't be controlled by corporate interests or persuasive commercials with a modern comedic edge. You can Botox your face but your butt will not be stopped.

Dear Gay Goddess please bless me with the relationship to my gender that any female dog enjoys. They are just like "pet me," and then, "I'm pregnant." It is not tender or meaningful, it requests no special recognition, and I appreciate that. A lady dog will go bonkers for a butt scratch. Wouldn't it be incredible if human moms just wanted a butt scratch? I would happily supply that. I sometimes swim at a pool and purposely go at the same time as a water aerobics class for pregnant women. I love that they all walk like earth movers, pushing their big bodies forward like a huge pile of dirt. Why is this burden on women? I'm sure lots of women consider bearing children an honor, and maybe if we lived in a matriarchal society it would be, but it seems like in this joint, the United States, bearing children just means your body gets ravaged with marks that our society hates, like loose skin and stretch marks and general exhaustion. So then you have to do the work of finding a way to truly love yourself when you didn't want to. None of my friends have kids. Some people from my high school do, but I don't really know them any-more. My instincts tell me it's an extraordinary, but truly unnecessary, experience. If it was earthier, dirtier, done in a jungle among smart people who just treated me like an ani-mal, I would consider it. Clearly I just don't want anything to make me too soft.

I'm sick of hearing myself think already. The past isn't anything except how you let it affect you today. Talk thera-py is bullshit. I don't know why being female makes me so mad when at the same time it's who I want to be. I just feel like there's this vast, gaping psychic vulnerability to being a woman. I don't want to soften more than I am. There is a pre-carious balance between how much I want to take care of ev-eryone I ever meet, and how much I want to smash my body into concrete by skateboarding my life away.

I need to remember to wear sunscreen. I just looked down at my arms and I am about twenty shades darker than the shade of my skin at birth. My skin health relies on a fleet of creams and broad-brimmed hats. Or does it? Centuries of people who didn't wear sunscreen have shuffled on and off life's stage. I guess they died younger and had an ozone layer. But sometimes I'm suspicious that the sunscreen thing is like the hydration thing—it's a good idea, but its impor-tance is overblown by bottled-water lobbyists and alarmist people who hate not having control over their longevity. It's a fucking hustle keeping your body reasonably healthy. I'm going to look like a vintage leather purse by the time I'm fifty years old.

My friend Kevin, a skateboarder I ride with at Potrero, told me about a pool at an abandoned motel off the 99. That route takes a little longer but it'll be worth it to hit this spot.

I watch for the exit and feel nervousness grow in my chest. A new pool is the most exciting place to approach. I don't know what the surface will be like, what the idiosyncrasies will be, if neighbors will call the cops on me or if I'll get to hang out for a while and figure it out.

I exit and take a left. There's a large Kia dealership in front of me. Cars. Great inventions. I find the block where the pool is supposed to be, and there are three abandoned motels in a row. I pull into the first, a one-story white sorta colonial-style dump with boarded-up windows and a giant dumpster in the parking lot. I don't see a pool so I turn down another row of rooms and I see two guys, a white one and a black one, probably in their early fifties, exchanging something. I think it's meth and that's because of the general reputation of this town and its valley, and the voluminous shorts both men are wearing. Each leg hole is as big as a grain silo. They both wear giant white T-shirts and giant white shoes, those fluffy generic athletic shoes you can get at any discount outlet. They are sad shoes. Is that classist? I just look at those shoes and think, "This stupid world and this body are so lumpy and hard to navigate that you ended up in this bozo zone of emotional pain which means gross drugs, uncomfortable living rooms, cigarettes, disappointed relatives and also you have to cover your feet. Another shitty reality in the toilet of life."

Maybe these dudes don't care about shoes. Probably they have more pressing concerns, like being high as fuck. I've seen drug problems in my family and friends and it usually isn't groceries or their sick mother they're worried about. It's all about the next good feeling, won't you stay with me just a little longer, perfect.

I don't look at the guys because I don't want to meet the eyes of sad addicts at an abandoned motel in a cruddy town in Central California. Don't invite the attention of the desperate who are not already your friend; that is my advice to you. I turn left onto the road and immediately turn into the next driveway. This is the joint. There is a pool inside a fence and an old Cadillac parked under a dying manzanita. My dad taught me the names of a ton of plants when I was little. I could barely string together a decent sentence but could point out my nearest Ceanothus 'Diamond Heights' easily. Kevin said there's a lady who lives in one of the abandoned rooms here. What does that mean? What do you do with no electricity and a hot room in the Central Valley? Is she old, or does she have some other thing going on? What does it smell like in there? What does she eat? I don't want to run into the lady. I hope she doesn't have a sick cat or something, because that would be sad. I only want to skate.

But what about when it's over a hundred degrees outside. How hot is it in her room? Does she just sit there and drip sweat, melting into her chair, skin flaccid and lying on her bones like rugs over guardrails? Is she used to being uncomfortable? Maybe she thinks this is life. She thinks life feels bad always and profound heat is just another way of experiencing that reality. What color is her skin? Not racially but sure, racially, but more like is it healthy? Radiant? Like a lotion commercial? No way. Maybe it's more like the windshield on her car. Fogged over with pollution, pollen and psychic detritus.

I throw my board over the fence and climb up the chain links. The top wobbles, because it doesn't have a stabilizing metal bar, but the give is minor and I jump to the ground with no major scrapes. I look into the pool and there's relatively little debris scattered about. Probably was skated recently. There is a shaded area with some worn wooden lounge chairs.

I descend into the shallow end of the pool using the steps. I love that absurdity. I jump onto my board and sail smoothly into the deep end. The transition is perfect. I huck myself up the back wall next to the light but not over it. I get spooked by the light when it's missing its cover. I don't want my wheel to get caught in the cobweb abyss of that empty hole. I'm sure I'd be fine but I haven't figured out how to mentally deal and throw myself at it.

Across the street is a car repair garage. Dudes mill about, move cars. I wonder if they ever notice activity over here and if they care. I don't get how a person lives in this town. I think I would be swallowed by malaise with all the meth and people hitting the lowest and saddest bottoms of their lives all the time. You would maybe become really happy about signs of life. Like a weed growing through a crack in the sidewalk. Instead of *kill it!* you would think, "You did it, little buddy! You didn't let the haters get you down." How could you ever be gay here? It feels like there are horrific murders just waiting to happen all over the place. I watch enough *48 Hours* to know it's not safe out here. Kids locked in closets, wives mixing antifreeze into their husband's iced tea every day, women found dismembered in garbage bags. And that's just the stuff I can think of. It has to get way worse.

The heat is getting me. I'm used to mild San Francisco, so this ninety-something degrees is a killer. I'm sweating through my clothes and feeling nauseous. Heat always makes me feel sick but I still hugely prefer it to the perpetual fog of San Francisco because it's better for my mood. I sit down to wait out the nausea and check my phone to see if Peter texted. Nothing. On one hand: of course. He has to focus on getting better. I can't do hard drugs. If I ever do coke with my friends, I know I will never ever come out of it and a whole horrific chapter of my life will open in which I'm just obsessed with cocaine and never get anything meaningful done and I will not be a success story. I will get sober and relapse, making everyone around me super depressed and there will be a relentless nagging guilt but then a stronger desire to do drugs and it will be like that *New York Times* writer David Carr who left his twin baby girls strapped into their car seats in a car in a snowstorm while he smoked crack inside some shitty house. Stability is precarious. Anyone can fall into this trap, just like even the smartest people can end up in a cult. We all have vulnerability holes and someone somewhere knows how to find them. No one is special.

My uncle Terrence was a heroin addict when I was growing up and I didn't know it. All I knew was he married this really hot punk lady from Berkeley and they both played bass in hardcore bands. We would drive down from Santa Rosa to meet them in Chinatown in San Francisco. We'd go to the shops and have dinner. I thought, "These are happy adult punks who must pay for things when I'm not looking because every time we leave a store they have stuff and I don't recall a transaction." Now I realize they were shoplifting. Who shoplifts from an already cheap store? Junkies. Really lovely, sweet, funny junkies who are your family and you happen to think they are the sexiest couple alive.

My uncle got sober when I was a senior in high school. My dad and a couple of his brothers went down to kidnap Terrence because he'd been trying to sober up and it never worked. He would come to our house for a weekend but leave after a day. Or, he would show up all beaten up because of drama between him and other drug people. I didn't really get it. His wife, Keiko, didn't want to get sober because she thought there wasn't a problem. So Terrence went to a recovery facility and we visited him on weekends. He seemed fine like any other time in his life so the point here is that apparently I have no intuition or general insight into a person's behavior. I'm sure he was a wreck and I just wanted him to be fine. After that he got an apartment in downtown Santa Rosa and I would run into him at punk shows in Guerneville. I would be watching a band, drinking from my flask, and then look to the back of the room and there he would be sitting alone in the shadows. Like a weirdo. We would wave to each other.

I'm lofting up a hip in the pool frontside when I hear a voice.

"No way, it's a girl!" the man voice says.

"Fuck yeah," someone else says who is also a man.

I jump off my board in the shallows and look to the men, who appear to be in their early twenties.

"Hi."

"You skate?" says one.

"What?"

"Right, duh, but I haven't seen a chick skate before."

"There are lots of us," I say.

"I haven't seen it, " he says, and I nod, because I believe him.

"A couple dudes are on their way, we're gonna film. You sticking around for a while?"

"I was planning to leave soon."

"Nah, you should stay! It would be rad to shred with a chick here!"

"Feels like a backhanded compliment," I kind of say, kind of mumble.

"What?"

"Nothing, I'll stay, sounds cool."

Slayer is, of course, blaring. No matter how much deeply satanic, heavy, brain-bashing music has been made since the early '80s, everyone seems to agree they did it best. It sets the appropriate mood.

It's somewhat awkward that when I skate with a boon of dudes, they are most often way better than me with regard to Skills Executed. Tricks. But that presumes you think tricks are the highest form of skateboarding, which I don't. Style is everything. Of *course* I would be pumped to be able to do crazy shit. But I'm just looking for frontside grinds on pool coping: loud, crunching, hammering noise from my trucks into the rarefied air next to the concrete. The ether that holds all the grace and insanity of the world. This is one great way of shouting into the void. Skating needs to be about letting go of my thoughts, not about obsessing over the particulars of a trick.

There are six guys here, all from Kerlin. Brown, white, the usual. Mostly in their twenties but a couple in their late thirties. Lifers on wide boards manufactured by small companies. There is a lot of "fuck yeah" and beer going down. When I skate they are somewhat quiet, because I think they're so used to saluting trophy moves that if someone just has soul without the peacock feathers, they don't know what to do.

I drop in and completely eat shit. Down on my left hip in a pile of cheap mops (my limbs). The drop-in is super steep and not really worth attempting, but I love a scary drop-in. The dudes go silent.

"Whoa," I say.

"You okay?" one of the guys—Carter—asks.

"Totally. Mind if I try that again?"

"Take it!"

Everyone is silent again as I set my tail on the coping. I

push my nose down and look forward, and stay on this time, though barely.

The night is warm and the only brightness is from lights the dudes brought, which are hooked up to a generator. The night sky outside our bubble is deep dark navy blue with lots of stars. It gives the feeling of being in a soft yet abusive egg. No one is around because the businesses are all closed. If the lady who lives in the room can hear us, she's not complaining.

"Dude, let's go to fucking Cheeks," a guy named Dragon says. I know right away he's talking about a strip club.

"Hell yeah, " says Oz.

Everyone packs their stuff up and no one looks at me, because I think they don't know how I'll react. They want to go ogle naked ladies, but they don't want me to shame them about it. Saying "Cheeks" in front of me is a dare: dare to object, dare to criticize. Dare to block their desire.

"I assume I'm invited," I say, smiling. My drive to prove them wrong overcomes my ambivalence about sitting in a boring strip club, wishing I had more money for tips. I'm a Consciousness Jesus: leading these dudes to imagine a world in which an intelligent woman may not object to objectification.

"Yeah man, you know where it is?" Oz asks me.

"No, but I can find it," I say.

"You a LEZ-bi-an?" Dragon asks.

"I'm an all-play," I say. "I've dated all the genders."

We let this statement sit comfortably for a moment.

I get in my car and allow a moment to consider that I am going to a strip club with a group of men I do not know. I don't live in this town. If I get drunk where will I stay? Will I make any weird choices and, like, blow someone or something? And then be filled with dread and anxiety every time

I think of it for the next thirty years? I did that once in high school. I was really drunk on Pabst and my parents were out of town. I had a bunch of people over and we decided to go pick up our friend Marco, who was this kinda crabby and up-tight musician dude. No one had ever seen him date a girl. I can't say I really know how it went down, but I do remember ending up in his room and giving him a blow job. I remem-ber him cumming in my mouth and then just hanging my mouth open over the carpeting and letting the jiz drip out. I made a sculpture in my high school art class of a woman's mouth with jiz dripping out and it did not go over well with my affable, mustachioed teacher. He looked exactly like the stereotype of a cop on desk duty. He winced when I described what it was. I can't believe I showed him my sculpture and said, "This is a head with sperm dripping out the mouth." So dissociative. I remember going back into the living room with Marco and acting like nothing happened and I think it was probably super obvious what happened. Maybe there were white splotches on my clothes. I remember seeing a guy sneer out of the drunk fractals of my eye. Horrifying. There are so many memories I wish I didn't have.

I drive to Cheeks and drink a beer in the car. There's a half-empty sleeve of smoked almonds stuffed in the back of a pocket in the door, so I dig those out and eat them. They actu-ally seem perfectly fine, even though I don't even remember when I left them there.

I park at Cheeks. I think of the movie *Thelma and Louise*. It was so good. I pull my sports bra out from under my shirt. It's oppressively tight. There is a cold sweat under my boobs. I have Wet Wipes in the car for cleaning my steering wheel so I take one and swab my armpits and the back of my neck. I try to reach down the back of my shirt because it's pretty sweaty there, too. I don't have a regular bra to put on so I just pull on a flannel and go inside, a little too warm.

The door guys look at my ID and lucky me, it's ladies' night, so I get in free. The transition from the outdoors, where air moves about freely and your mind can expand, into the stagnant canned air of the indoors is hard to take. I wave to the dudes, who are all sitting in swivel chairs next to the stage. Carter is the only one who sees me, and he waves back. I wonder if this was a good idea. Do I want to be here? I can't tell. I don't have to work tomorrow.

I order a vodka soda for fifteen stupid dollars and then hit the cash machine next to the bar. It reeks like farts over there. I would like to think there's a farting station for men at a strip club but you know most guys wouldn't extend the courtesy of using it.

I sit down with the dudes, closest to Carter. He seems like the nicest one.

"Is this weird?" he says.

"Strip clubs?" I ask.

"Yeah, like being a girl at a strip club."

"First of all, I am a woman, if you haven't noticed," I tease him.

"Oh shit I . . ."

"I'm just messing with you. I don't know, it's not bad, but it is kind of strange, because I don't want a lap dance or anything, but I do feel obligated to give the women a lot of money because like, look at what they're doing. It's so nuts. I could never do that." I point to the lady onstage who is undulating like a giant ocean wave. She's wearing a black bikini with fluorescent green pot leaves on it. She walks over to me and squats with her knees open so her vagina in its suit is at my eye level. It makes me feel so weird. I want to admire what is happening so she that feels good but also I don't instinctively want this view or general experience. I choose to dig a couple dollar bills out of my pocket and hand them to her. She takes them with her boobs. Carter looks flushed. Why is everything so sexual. Oh, because we're at a strip club. Damn it.

I guess Oz and Dragon were also watching the dance I got. I don't think any of them are ponying up too much money for the ladies. Dragon says, "You see her lips?"

"Ew," I say.

"I wanna get over *that* box," Oz says, trying to make a hilarious double-entendre with the lady and also the fact of carving over the death box in a pool while skateboarding.

"Jesus, you guys," I say, with a joking tone that also invokes being grossed out. "You're killing me."

"Never gets old," Oz says.

"Aw, you don't like to talk about stinky pink?" Dragon prods. "I like slash."

Carter laughs, then looks at me, then looks back at the stage. I feel sick in a very familiar way. I gulp my drink down and signal a waitress for another.

A gorgeous girl sits down next to me. She has long black hair with braids and ribbons hanging in it. The ribbons are light blue and pink, and look kind of like how Bootsy Collins does his hair but a little more orderly. She has the longest black eyelashes, and she does that thing of tilting her head down and looking up at me. She's wearing a farm girl outfit. Her halter top is pink-and-white gingham with white lace trim, and her hot pants match. Her steep wedges have the same gingham pattern plus big bows on the toes. When I get around girls like this I feel like such a man, and I'm really not gender dysphoric or anything. I just don't understand this screaming Barbie version of female. How did they learn to walk in those things? What kind of girl camp did I miss and why?

"So, how are you tonight?" She smiles and sips a pink drink. A fresh cocktail materializes next to me and I grab it hungrily.

"Oh, I'm good. You know." I feel giddy and encumbered by my limbs. I feel myself listing left so I counterbalance by leaning on the arm of my chair.

"Are you visiting from out of town?"

"I live in San Francisco, so kind of but not really." I start laughing even though it's not a joke.

"That's super funny," she says.

"I was skating with these guys and coming to a strip club just felt natural after getting gross and sweaty." I'm saying words just to fill the air. I feel like such a dummy. "I'm buying you a lap dance," I say to Carter.

"Wait really?" He looks totally confused.

"Yep." God I am being so weird.

"You don't even know me," he says.

"Shut up, dude, just be stoked!" Dragon slurs and claps him on the back. "Where's mine?"

"I got this one, someone else has to cover yours," I say, and give the lady a wad of bills. At least I have the money to cover this, which I wouldn't have two weeks ago. After buying Carter this lap dance I immediately regret it. Who deals with their nervous energy by spending a hundred dollars on someone they don't know?

The next song is kind of lame, it's a slow metal song. The stripper, Veronica, leads Carter off for his dance.

The song changes and a new dancer comes out. She zooms up the pole, clamps on with her ankles and spins down with her knees out like a butterfly. I like these acts of athletic excellence.

There is a crew of business dudes across the stage from me. There is a glance of hard appraisal from these men. The dancer strides over and puts her butt toward them, then bends over and enhances their view with her movement. One of the guys reaches a finger up and snaps her G-string right around the top of her crack. She glares at him and walks away. I jump up and push through many wheeled chairs to get to them.

"The *fuck*, man!" I yell. Heavy chairs covered in pleather push against my thighs and it feels like trying to run in three feet of water. My pants slide down my ass but I'm so focused on the finger man I half yank them up with one hand and pull myself forward with the other. Finger Fingerson tries to act cool like nothing happened though even in this doldrum light I can see he is red-faced and uncomfortable. Maybe that should have been enough for me, if I just cared about him learning his lesson, but it's not.

"Hey dude! Keep your hands off the girls!" Could I have thought of something a little less pimp-y? I keep one hand on a table to stay upright.

"It's cool, it's cool," he says and tips his beer toward me to signal "We're good."

"It's cool with *you* maybe, but it's not cool *in the world*," I scream.

"Are you serious, bitch? Hey! Can somebody help me out here?" Fingerling Potatoes looks around wildly for back-up. His face is pinched and calculating. I finally get to him and grab the lapel of his suit like we're in a movie.

"You wanted a woman to touch you, right?" I holler. "Look, dream come true. All consensual. Now get the fuck out of here."

"Alright miss," a deep voice booms behind me and a fat hand grabs my shoulder. I lurch to the left, falling on all fours onto that disgusting carpeting. I look up to see a tall security dude with a goatee reaching down to grab the back of my shirt and next thing you know I am upright again, trying to arrange my feet on the floor. "You need to leave now." Carter is right behind this enormous man, a Dumpster full of boulders.

"And that fucking ass man gets to stay?" I point at the guy I was trying to humiliate and slap the security guy's arm, not very hard. "He was grabbing the girls. He has to leave."

"None of your business ma'am, let's just move out now." With an iron grip on my collar he pushes me, and I walk like a puppet. A few people stare but most just continue with their lives.

"Come on now, she's with me, I'll take her out," Carter's voice filters through the music and conversation. Ham hands just keeps walking. "Dude. Hello?" My escort ignores him completely and delivers me to the front door where he gives me a little shove in the shoulder. I stumble then turn around and look at the bouncer. He gives me a cartoonish smile and a wave made of big schnitzel fingers.

Carter finds me sitting on a parking block. Gravel and cigarette butts pool at my feet, and a little bug with a pincer on its behind wiggles around. A couple tall street lights illuminate the lot. I see a head shop across the street. It has a tastefully simple neon sign that says, "SMOKE SHOP." Carter rubs his eyes with his palm and laughs. He shakes his head. His dark brown hair flips across his forehead and he loses his balance and tips backward off the curb. Now I'm laughing and we both lose it on this filthy spot. There's a small patch of grass behind us that I'm sure is all hobo pee and broken glass. We writhe around in the grossness of this spot, flailing arms and kicking. Like siblings in a pile of leaves. I deliver a few small punches to Carter's chest, I want him to play with me like a puppy. He jabs at me. We're small sun bears who can't help provoking each other. Abruptly the vibe feels flirtatious. I haven't had sex with anyone in months, so maybe I would? I can't decide. It creates so much BS to get involved with another human. I've by and large successfully sworn off dating. I'm not sure I know what I like anymore. Historically, I just date whoever likes me. They always turn out to be alcoholics. Carter and I laugh and hiccup and then a different door guy comes around and says we have to leave.

We walk past an enormous white SUV that's hemorrhaging fancy-dressed people in their early twenties. They stream over to Cheeks like ants. A girl glances at us and giggles and says, "Whoa." I guess we look messy. Then she turns and tip-taps along with her friends in high silver heels and tiny jeans. I try to imagine what she looks like naked with such small hips. It baffles me to see such small adults. I bet she has the tiniest vagina.

"You owe me a lap dance," Carter grins. "I was just getting started and then you had to play super hero from Feminism 101. You sounded just like my sister. Hey let's go get rolling papers at that head shop."

We cross the street and pass into the bong zone. Long, scratched-up glass cases hold myriad bongs of all shapes. At the back of the room is a doorway with a heavy black felt curtain hanging over it. There's a paper sign taped above the door that says, "Joy Story." I walk directly through the curtain.

I almost bump into a table that has a display of novelty pasta. You can get penis shapes or boob shapes. I imagine bachelorette parties of rapturous drunk ladies using plastic forks to spear long chains of penis pasta in red sauce.

I walk over to a wall of dildoes of all colors. Neon green, hot pink, shaped like a dolphin, marbleized silicone shaped like a torpedo. Butt plugs of all sizes, from the negligible to the unimaginable. Carter sidles up next to me. "That's a . . . pretty big arm," he says about a silicone fist.

"Yeah, I guess I don't feel drawn to that one, but I respect the people who are," I say.

There's a rack of clothing I have to check out. "Whoa! Super sexy!" I holler through the store and pull out two outfits made out of clear plastic wrap–type material, one in each hand. The lady one has a pink bow at the neck and some bunched-up plastic that I think is supposed to look like lace. The man job has a black bow-tie and some flimsy stitching that wants to look like a tuxedo. They embody the embarrassment of sex for me. One time an ex of mine begged me to wear a cheerleader uniform for him. We argued about it for a week and then I gave in. I mean, I really do want to turn on whoever I'm sleeping with. I let him get one for me. It was a size too small. When I put it on I never felt less like myself in my whole life. The waist of the skirt cut into me like a dull butter knife. Wide red and white panels of polyester shot off my hips. The little vest rode up on me and exposed the sausage roll of my middle. I walked out into the living room and let my boyfriend at the time, Jim, see me. I tried not to look as horrible as I felt. I sat on his lap and we had sex and I made him sign a typed contract that he would never ask me to wear it again.

I know this is weird, but what I feel sexy in is a big pair of cotton granny panties. I think if they hang just right at my hips, that's hot. I think a shitty old tank top is sexy. I guess I just love anything mundane. Very subtle cues of line and proportion. I like when a person has some extra pounds on them. I like when their pants don't quite fit right. I despise arrogance and prejudice.

"We have to get these," Carter grabs a couple suckers

shaped like boobs and throws them on the worn linoleum check-out counter where a bored twentysomething butch girl is sitting and reading a fat book. It says "BUKOWSKI" in thick, uppercase letters down the spine. She looks up with shaggy dirty-blonde hair hanging in sleepy brown eyes and regards the pile of boob suckers.

"Those are pretty cool," she says and goes back to reading. She peeks up at us one more time, takes some mental notes, and goes back to her book.

"Really seems like you're hitting on me," I say to Carter.

"Is that okay?" Carter asks.

"Yeah," I say slowly. I think I do want to see where this goes. "Let's go somewhere else and have another drink though." I can feel myself fading and plus I'm not ready to face being naked. Carter pays for the candy and we walk out. There is an inflatable sheep hanging from the ceiling, so I jump up and bat it.

"Don't do that," the counter girl says drolly.

We walk out into the night and Carter looks down the street. "There's a place called Henry's, it's a piano bar," he says. "It's a gay bar."

"Sounds good to me." We link arms and weave down the sidewalk to Henry's. I like the feeling of my arm intertwined with his. The rush, the uncertainty. Henry's has no windows and a huge bear of a door guy sitting on a tiny stool. "Bear on a unicycle," I say.

"What's that?"

"Nothing."

We order beers. We sit on tall chairs next to a narrow drink ledge and a long mirror. We each take huge gulps of our drinks, and an older gay dude walks over, sipping something clear through a tiny red straw.

"Hi," he says, with a long dip to the 'i' and a wink.

"Hello," Carter says, and gives a "cheers" clink with his glass.

"Have you two been here before?" the man asks.

"No," I say. "I don't live here, though."

"Where are you from?"

"San Francisco."

"Oh! The big city. So are you two together?"

We look at each other.

"We just met today," I say.

"Oh," the guy says. "Well, you're very cute together."

"Thank you," we both say, and he walks away.

"Are your friends going to worry about you?" I ask.

"Nah, I texted Oz and let him know I would see them tomorrow."

"Cool," I say. I feel a little shy. I'm not immune to the shot of dopamine in my blood. Even though this is a one-night thing and I am certain I'll never talk to Carter again, I feel a soft rush of attraction.

"I hope you plan on staying at my place tonight. We don't actually have to have sex just because you're staying over." A huge smile breaks across his face. His dark brown eyes light up. He has thick, black eyebrows that are almost a mono-brow. His shoulders are somewhat naturally broad, though he's not overly muscled on the top half of his body, like most skaters. I like how skateboarders exist in their bodies, like they know they're permeable, they're not bracing against getting hurt because they know it's inevitable.

"I do want to stay with you. I can't put into words what I want to happen there, can we just see how it goes?"

"Yeah," he smiles. I look down at my drink. A disco ball kicks in overhead. A drag show starts.

We're on Carter's bed making out. He's laid back on his bed and I'm leaning over and straddling him. It's hot. His room is a gross mess. There are tools, skateboards, trucks, wheels, shoe boxes and more random crap everywhere. He has a plastic lawn furniture chair at a crappy Ikea desk with mountains of papers on it and an ancient Dell laptop. He starts pulling my shirt up when his doorbell rings. It rings and rings and rings and him kissing me doesn't make it stop. We also hear his phone blowing up. He finally pulls away and yells *"Fuck!"* As he leaves the room he sticks his head back in. "When I get back, I'm getting that shirt off." I feel myself blush, and pull the shirt back down over my waist. I lie back and let my head spin with booze.

I stay in Carter's room, assuming he'll get rid of whoever is there. I hear the other guys we skated with inside the house. A few minutes pass. I don't know what to do. It seems so embarrassing to go out there. I feel really drunk anyway. I look at my phone, and Peter has sent several texts.

"Paloma?"

"Hello?"

"ARE YOU ALIVE?"

"Seriously though are you okay?"

I write him back. "Dude. I'm fine. I'm in Kerlin."

He immediately responds. "Why the hell are you in that shithole?"

"Skated today."

"Isn't it dark out?"

"Yeah. I'm at some dude's house."

"Is he cool? You're not texting me from the trunk of his car, right?" Pete knows I'm obsessed with murder.

"I'm playing with the spare tire in the boot of a Geo Spectrum."

"So all's good."

"Yep! I'll text you tomorrow."

Carter is still in the living room. That feels kind of rude? I want to leave and just drive to San Francisco, but I probably shouldn't. I'm definitely drunk, and even driving from Cheeks to Carter's house was a bad idea.

I step out his bedroom door into the living room. The dudes are all around a coffee table and my sight is blurry but it looks like there are lines of cocaine cut up, a pair of scissors, an ATM card and straws. Carter jumps up and runs to my side. The guys look surprised and I know they'll grill Carter when I'm gone.

"Hey, you want some water?" he says, steering me toward the kitchen. "These guys won't be here long, you don't mind, right? I mean, you're welcome to join us if you want."

"Nah."

"Are you mad?"

"What? No. I just wish I could go home."

"No no, don't go home! Seriously just give me ten minutes then these guys will leave."

I go back into Carter's room and shut the door. I sit on the end of the bed and sip the water. Some of it spills on my sweatshirt. The water traveling down my booze-coated throat tastes sour. I hate how uncomfortable I am. I want to turn the page to tomorrow. But I can't. I just have to get through tonight. I wish I hadn't decided to bone down with this guy. This is why I stay away from dating and just skate. It always gets weird and uncomfortable. I end up in situations that just weren't worth it. Maybe if I just sleep a bit I can sober up and leave.

At 5:30 in the morning I wake up and I am still alone in the bed. I walk out into the living room and Carter is cleaning up. There are many crushed Modelo cans everywhere, piles of cigarette butts, and one dumb square of mirror sitting on the coffee table. Carter smokes a cigarette and washes some dishes.

"Hey," I say. "I'm going to head out."

"Aw, fuck, really? I was gonna be in there in just a second." Carter turns the sink off and comes toward me. I take a step back.

"Yeah, I shouldn't have stayed. I don't even know you."

"Can I call you sometime?"

"Sure." I guess I expected him to be more apologetic, or to try harder to get me to stay. I won't talk to him later but it's easier to just say okay and know that worst-case scenario, I'll just ignore one call. Though most likely, he'll just skip it and I'll be relieved.

I let myself out the front door. The daylight is abusive to my eyes and stomach. My car sits with the driver's window fully open but fortunately no one touched it. I head to San Francisco, all the windows down, music off, and try to let my senses air out. Wisps of my dirty hair blow around my face. I feel like a dumbass. I should have continued on my own adventure and not gotten sidetracked with these weird dudes that just led me to spend too much money on strippers and booze. I have better things to do, like build my business empire. I head to Irma's house.

I fall asleep at Irma's in the morning, and she goes out to walk dogs. By two in the afternoon I can't sleep anymore, so I decide to go for a run while I wait for Irma to get home.

I chug up to the entrance to Bernal Park where I begin a slow ascent up the little dirt trail next to the big paved area. To my right I can see over all the Mission and Noe Valley. Little cubes that are people's houses, broccoli heads that are trees, and streets. There is one guy walking down the hill with three small terriers that crisscross each other's paths and smell every inch of pavement and earth. There's a trail leading to a sidewalk down the south side of the hill; I mince-run down the steep dirt and pass a guy wearing one of those things that holds your baby on your chest.

I start walking down the top part of the sidewalk so as to preserve my knees. There's a plastic cookie jar shaped like a dog perched on the corner of a white picket fence and a note below it with a color photo of a fluffy, smiling golden retriever. It says:

Please give your dog a treat!
Our sweet pooch Clara died peacefully
In her sleep one week ago.
She was fourteen years old.

As I read this, my eyes tear up. I keep reading the part that says "peacefully in her sleep" over and over. I continue down the hill. I stare at the pavement in front of me because tears are sliding down my cheeks. Hangovers are so stupid. Everything feels so emotional. I cross Cortland Avenue and head up a small incline to Holly Park. By the time I'm on my way back up Bocana I'm not crying anymore. I pass a really old guy with white hair who is sweeping the sidewalk. He looks up at me and says, "They went that way about an hour ago," and points up the hill. I think he's joking but also sort of wonder if there was a pack of running people he thinks I belong to. I smile and continue my bouncy climb, mostly on the balls of my feet because the upward angle of the street is so ridiculous. I'm not sure if that's good form or not.

I do a couple more laps around the hill and Holly Park then head down Folsom Street to do a lap around Precita Park. There is a rottweiler a few yards ahead of me who appears not to have an attendant human. At Precita the dog abruptly takes a sharp left into traffic and I yell "No!" and as he looks back at me a dark green Mustang grazes, but does not hurt him. He continues across the road and the lady driving the Mustang looks at me disapprovingly. I follow the dog up the road whistling every dog-summoning whistle I can think of but he won't let me catch him. He takes a right on Shotwell toward the six lanes of heavy traffic on Cesar Chavez Street. There are so many cars and I yell "No!" again and he turns his head to look at me but keeps going forward and this time a bus clips his shoulder. I can't tell if it hurt him because he launches up the street in shock and I follow him yelling "No, no, no!" He won't let me get close and he tries to cross the street again but gets out of the way of a white Subaru just in time. He is running along toward Mission Street and I don't think there is any way I can stop him. At Mission Street it will be heavy and fast traffic in all directions. I feel like I'm pushing him forward by chasing him and the thought of this dog getting hit by a car is too much so I quit running and watch for a second then turn around and head back to Irma's house. I can't help him and I can't see him get killed. I feel kind of crazy. I get to Irma's house and crack a beer, then unfurl her yoga mat to do some stretching.

Irma and I saunter up to a little theater on Mission Street to see a comedy show. We've each stored two Pabst tall boys in our jackets, since there's no bar. We walk inside to a messy foyer. One crappy couch and a makeshift table with an enormous dude sitting behind it taking money. We pay five bucks each and go inside a small black box theater to sit. Half the chairs are broken or ripped up and spilled on. It's particularly low attendance tonight, probably because of the rain.

We watch a solidly okay show. The hosts were actually funnier than the guests. At the end of the scheduled performers they pick two names out of a hat to do three-minute sets. I decide to put my name in the hat. I don't know if I can pull it off but it's also pretty low-stakes to be in a room of so few people and bomb.

Since there's only about twelve people here, my name is called. The host, a tall, kinda thick white dude with yellow glasses like John Goodman in *The Big Lebowski* calls me up and shakes my hand.

"Hey what's up. I'm Paloma, and the visual cues are probably telling you right now, I'm a woman. You into that?"

There is a very small "*woo*" from the three people who decide to participate.

"Did you know that I can wrap my tiny hands around the pink handles of the Master's Tools as they're sold at Home Depot, and I can take these tiny hammers and pliers and mess up some ladies, right? No one can make fun of women as well as I can. I know all the internal secrets. I'm a secret weapon. I'm an ancient recipe, like macaroni and cheese. I am anxiety frozen in a block of ice in Greenland waiting for a curious nerd with a pickaxe to find me."

Zero enthusiasm from the audience. I know I'm being completely terrible and obtuse but the worse I am, the more amped up I get inside. I plow on.

"Given recent events in the higher offices of our nation, the instillation of a dangerous plutocrat, a demagogue, I feel it's important to consider our own individual weaponization. As in being the bomb you want to throw, to paraphrase the Lesbian Avengers. As in graphic novel shit when your arm is a machine gun and one of your eyeballs is an outer planet with undiscovered water. This Otherbeast, in a rare moment of repose, allows a romantic prospect or thoughtful child to open the refrigerator-like door to its torso and they see, where the heart should be, a canary on a swing."

"Weird," one guy says loudly, firmly, but not unkindly.

"Yeah. I can tell I'm being weird. Okay. Comedy! You know what? I need to work on my set. Thanks for letting me get up here." I say and I go back to my seat. I'm shaking inside. I know I was awful. But I enjoyed it in a really strange way.

Irma and I walk up Mission Street in a light rain. "You did a good job," she says.

"I didn't, but I'm okay with it," I say. "I didn't really make anyone laugh. I don't even know if comedy is my thing. But I might try it a few more times."

"Yeah but there's something there. *You* were in there. You have to keep that part, the thing that is the weird you and just figure out how to commit to it and sustain it for however long you're onstage."

"That's a nice way to say it."

"I know."

"Do you ever feel completely horrible about the people you've slept with and dated?"

"No. There's been a lot of shit that didn't work out, but you know. That's how it's gotta be."

"But are you saying that because you know it's the right thing to say or do you really feel that way?"

"What else can I do? Feeling bad about my dates is hating myself. They were cool chicks. Didn't mean it had to be forever. I don't really want forever. I don't know if I'm capable of that. I don't know if 'forever' is even natural." Irma puts her arm around me. "You feeling bad?"

"I always feel bad."

"Your mind moves too fast."

"I know. Even that makes me feel terrible."

"Aw, tortured little dude!"

"Is this life? You just feel bad sometimes and good sometimes and then you're always doing something except when you're sleeping?"

"I never thought about it but yeah, I think that's it."

By now we're far down Mission Street, past Chavez. We duck into El Rio for a drink, and to sit outside in the dumb cold. Irma finds us a spot while I grab drinks.

The bartender trips me out. She looks exactly like this girl who was my nemesis in junior high. Her real name was Olivia Johns, so of course everyone asked if she was named after the singer Olivia Newton-John. She was not. She had perfectly feathered honey blonde hair parted down the middle, long skinny legs in tight high-waisted Levi's and heavy eyeliner. She decided she didn't like me one day in that way that thirteen-year-old girls do. She was considered very pretty at our school, and held a lot of social power. I never understood why people got excited about her. When she decided she didn't like me, all my friends followed her. The only people who were nice to me were also in band. Suddenly no returned smiles or greetings, people canceled plans, whispered and smiled coyly when I walked by. A couple days into this, Olivia passed me in the hallway between classes and said, "I'll see you outside after school." I knew this meant we were going to fight. Our entire junior high was talking about it. I was terrified. Chrissy Entenmann, who had stolen my Swatch in gym class and brazenly wore it in front of me, also passed and said, "You're in trouble." I couldn't concentrate in class and had no idea how I would handle it.

I took as long as I could gathering my books after school. I walked outside and it looked like all three hundred kids from my junior high were waiting. There was an old Camaro parked along the curb and a guy, a senior in high school, Olivia's boyfriend, leaned out and yelled, "I wanna see some blood!" I walked over to Olivia.

"So what do you want?" I asked.

"You said you had forty dollars at Easter and you really had eighty." she accused.

"I don't remember how much I had."

She had a couple other beefs that I can't remember, but I do sense that they were all class-based issues that boiled down to "You're a rich girl and you won't admit it."

I told her I didn't know what to say, and she got angry and called me a weasel who thought I could get out of anything. I recall hearing her boyfriend egg her on from his car. We stood and looked at each other, then Olivia pushed me. I started falling backwards and instinctively grabbed her forearms to hold myself up. Her hands wrapped around my forearms. She narrowed her eyes and dug her long nails into my flesh. I had scars from her nails for years.

She spewed some insults at me and then walked away. I walked home crying my eyes out. Olivia and her friends—including a boy who had been my boyfriend at the time—would follow me home every single day for weeks, throwing rocks at me and calling me names. None of my friends would talk to me, so I made other friends who were kind, and much less fickle. I cried every single day of my life after that, often multiple times, until my sophomore year in high school. One day after school I abruptly realized I hadn't cried in a couple days and was relieved, thinking that profoundly painful time might be passing. Like an asshole, once my old shitty friends stopped being mad at me, I rejoined their friend group and left the good ones behind. I'm so ashamed of that choice.

To this day I don't trust cliques. I don't trust groups of friends that feel powerful, or that feel like their connection actively excludes others. I've had friends from lots of different crews ever since then. People are often cruel, and almost all of them want to elect a most popular person and vie for their attention. It's disgusting. We don't all need to be Kennedys. We don't all need an Olivia Johns.

I dip into a despondent hole thinking about this stuff. I walk outside with our drinks.

"Hey buddy!" Irma says and I snap out of it. I sit down and give her a big hug for no reason.

Pete tells me he can have someone come down to meet me in the East Bay and refresh my supply in the next day or two. I want to see him in person, though, get a feel for where he's at after detox. Is it delusional for me to think he can work at the farm and stay clean and sober? It doesn't seem so nuts to me. It's just weed, I don't think of it as a drug, or a dangerous one anyway. Plenty of sober alcoholics are bartenders. Marijuana is much better than booze. Plus hard drugs are prohibited on the land; they're bad vibes, and this is a workplace. You can't mix the two. I'm sure some of the trimmers do molly or mushrooms or whatever on their off time. But Pete's been on a merry little seesaw of heroin and meth. What a nightmare. I'll never touch that stuff.

Peter texted me when he got out of the detox place a week ago. He just said, "Heading home." I feel apprehensive about seeing him. I keep catching myself holding my breath and wonder when I last inhaled. I guess I'm afraid for him to see that I want him to stay safe so desperately; it feels unbearably vulnerable. Like he'll want to crush me just for wanting him to stay alive, for wanting anything at all that puts pressure on him to survive in a certain way. How do I shoulder the guilt of not being an addict like him? It's embarrassing to be able to drink booze and smoke weed reasonably when I know he doesn't have that option.

Sometimes I think my drinking might be an issue. I can't tell. So many people are worse off than me. Can you have survivor's guilt when the object of your guilt is alive? I know the chances of him staying sober are slim. It hasn't worked so far. Maybe I just hate myself for wanting him to stay clean when I know that's most likely a losing proposition.

For this visit, I want to stay at a very corporate hotel with a long hallway and an impermeable industrial carpet leading to my room. I want to ride in an unthinkably slow elevator lined with posters for the hotel restaurant featuring an over-lit taco salad and a jaunty lady drink in a martini glass. Women with soft waves in their hair, leaning against boring dudes who have used deodorant since they were seven years old, laughing. Cheap wall sconces and framed corporate art. Soft color tones everywhere. Customers with long, hemmed jean shorts and big, white, off-brand sports shoes, the kind that aren't designed for any actual sport or movement beyond riding a lawn mower and affixing pegboard to the wall of your garage. *Maybe* for walking a purebred family dog or riding a cruiser bicycle with a large seat.

Pete texts me about going to a comedy show. That could be perfect because then we don't have to talk a lot and maybe I'll get some inspiration for how to retool my set. He said Rigo is coming too, so it will be like a work function except we're all in a bar and my brother just got out of detox. Good evening, Norman Rockwell.

The bar is a bar. What can I say? It's divided into two sides, one with the comedy stage and the other with bar sports like pool, pinball and shuffleboard (and drinking, but I didn't need to say that). I walk in and find my brother sitting at the bar on the comedy side. He's drinking a pint of dark beer.

"Hi!" I say.

"What up," he says and gives me a one-armed side hug.

"Just re-toxifying yourself?" I ask, pointing at his beer.

He looks at me without a word. My face flushes with frustration and embarrassment. I swallow an ocean of disappointment, like bodysurfing and missing a wave, getting tossed and held under by violently undulating salt water. He's not going to stay clean. I'm a fucking idiot for hoping otherwise.

"How are you feeling?" I ask.

"Good."

"Are you on some kind of regimen to help your body go through the detox?"

"I'm out of detox, dummy. It's done, I'm good."

"Oh, I . . ."

"I don't want to talk about it."

"You should consider therapy."

"Shut the fuck up. If you want to be here with me, shut the fuck up."

Tears spring to my eyes and I try to keep my voice steady as I order a drink. I sit and try to focus on the stage but my body is vibrating with stress. A short guy with glasses adjusts the mic and looks to the back of the room, giving a thumbs-up.

Rigo shows up after the show has started. We watch from the bar. He gives me a big hug and kisses my cheek, which I know is him being grateful for the crazy amount of weed I'm selling on his behalf. His affection momentarily brings me back into my body but then I get right back on edge.

There aren't a ton of people here for the show, maybe twenty-five or so. The host brings up Rigo's friend, James.

"Word, nice to see everybody, I'm James, fucking great to be here, man," James starts. "I'm gonna get right into it. Do I have any guys here who are dating a woman with daddy issues?" He shields his eyes and looks into the crowd. A couple men raise their hands. "It's crazy, right? I got this chick, she's cool, but she like wants to call me 'Daddy' when we're in bed gettin' nasty. It was cool at first but then I met her dad. She introduced me and I was like, am I really being compared to this balding dude who's got like a full-on war going on with his neighbor's lawn? He's walking by the neighbor's house, shooting Roundup at this fluffy fucking grass, putting swastikas and shit in his design of burned grass, and I'm like, that's not sexy. You calling me 'Daddy' isn't sexy, and now it's off-limits." The crowd goes nuts. I don't get it. I mean, I know this is a way of making jokes and that people say dumb stuff like this. But I do wish I could grill every person in here including James about why exactly this is hilarious. It just pisses me off so hard that women are the scaffolding for so much ridicule, and the point of so many jokes is that a woman is, or women are, stupid. My anger boils up inside me until I feel like I want to shove every glass off the bar and hear it shatter. I want to slam my own head onto the bar until I'm bleeding and sick with regret.

"I'll be back," I say to Pete and Rigo, then go outside. I walk down the sidewalk. What's the point of me trying to do comedy when dumb shits like that guy get onstage and always get laughs? No one wants anything different than that. Maybe a small group of feminists does. Maybe I just need a decent group of five friends and I can cleverly word my thoughts and have them laugh and that's enough. I don't need to try and get paid—though when I think that, I realize I don't think comics ever get paid. You're supposed to be grateful any gaggle of idiots at a bar will look at you for five minutes and laugh. If that's not a dynamic perfectly drawn for a child of alcoholics, I don't know what is.

A girl skates by me on a wide '80s board with soft wheels. I think it's a Psycho Stick. She's wearing fat bunny slippers and boxer shorts, even though it's kinda cold out. Also a hoodie and a hat with cat ears. I involuntarily smile. Now *that* is comedy. A self-possessed woman who does not give a shit. Not some dumbass guy whose friends laughed at one thing he said one time and now he thinks he should be a stand-up comedian. This lady is a genius. I keep walking. There are all sorts of seeds or berries or something on the ground from the kind of tree that's planted all along the street. They squish under my shoes. I pass a few people but don't look anyone in the eye. I need to just go back to my hotel and chill with some *Dateline* and a drink. I leave without saying goodbye to the dudes. I know they'll survive without me.

I get to the farm to re-up on product and there's only one truck there, Rigo's. I had expected to see Peter, since he's supposed to be working. The house's energy feels strange as I walk up. There's not a single person outside on a break or any sign of life whatsoever. When I get inside, there's no one around, just the dumpy sectional couch and glass coffee table, somehow looking abandoned. I walk into the trim room and see Rigo rummaging through a pile of plastic paint tubs. He looks up and asks if I've talked to my brother before he even says hello.

"I got a text from him saying not to come over, but he didn't say why and didn't respond to any more texts. I can't go back to L.A. if I'm not supplied so I came anyway."

"We were robbed last night. Your brother is out talking to a few people and buying cameras and other shit," he says. "I chewed him the fuck out though. He's been lax as fuck with installing our security system. He started using again, you know that, right?"

"I gathered."

"I made him go to detox. He didn't want to. Fucking idiot."

"He told me he went but didn't explain what was up."

"He was nodding out in his office. Slacking. That shit'll kill him."

"I know."

"Whatever happens with your brother, your job is safe. You're doing great. So don't sweat his shit."

"Oh. Thank you. I really kind of love it."

"Well, keep it up. I just need to figure out what we do about this robbery shit, if anything. They got a bunch of money we were about to bury. Shoulda fuckin' stayed late and handled it but I needed a goddamn break."

"I didn't know you guys buried money."

"Most people do. Just a bunch of paint cans." He briefly smiles. "Friend of mine used to bury his money in grocery bags until rats ate it all. Funny as fuck thinking about rats shitting out all that money. Dude was bummed."

"How much was stolen from here?"

"Fuckers got thirty thousand in cash and gold. And the tubs of trim we had waiting to ship."

"Holy shit. What should I do?"

"Don't worry about it. Come back in a couple days and we'll put together a package for you to take south. Peter should be back tonight. Everyone else is back tomorrow afternoon."

I feel creeped out by the farm. The vibe is fucked up by the robbery. It feels like waking up too many days in a row super hungover. Like there's a film of evil over everything.

"What about getting a safe?"

"We're doing that."

"So, where's Pete?"

"In town."

When I finally get reception on my phone again I text Peter. No response. I don't understand why he can't just be consistent. Why is that so hard? He and my dad have that same cranky moody volatile thing. One minute they're the most affable, fun people you've ever met and the next minute, storm clouds roll in and they're vicious. Growing up my dad would get really drunk then get super affectionate with me, like he'd suddenly have this big moment of thinking I was the best thing that ever happened. I could see a loving feeling rise up in him, perfect like a freshly cut watermelon, and he would come to smother me in a hug that always pushed my head at a weird angle and hurt my neck. It was a hug purely about his enjoyment, grabbing a moment of feeling good. The impact on me was not a consideration; I was supposed to be grateful. I should have carried a body pillow surrogate. If I didn't want to be touched or was just generally averse to a wasted dad finding an affection for me that could have just as easily been directed at a good steak or cheese plate, he would immediately call me a bitch and do a dismissive head shake and flick of the wrist first perfected by drag queens imitating Elizabeth Taylor in *Who's Afraid of Virginia Woolf?* Love to disgust in two seconds flat. I get that he just wanted to feel good, like we all do. But no one's body should be disrespected in that process. I know that sounds pedantic but if you really dig in to reality, it's a sadly radical concept.

Rigo looks at his phone. "Hey, I just got a text from a friend in town, and he's saying Peter is at The Redwood and I should get there immediately. Can you go and see what the fuck is up with that asshole?"

I drive to the motel with a bad feeling in my gut. When I get close I see lights spinning atop an ambulance, and first responders moving between the vehicle and one of the rooms. I slow down and stare and I see my brother's car. My heart freezes. I pull into the driveway of the motel and as the gurney pulls out of the room I see Peter on it. There are people around him and I can't tell what is happening. I jump out of my car and run over and when I'm almost to the stretcher ask very loudly, "Is he alive?"

A lady EMT says, "Yes. Are you family?"

"Yes."

"You can meet us at Mad River Hospital, do you know where that is?"

"I'll find it."

My stupid brother is in a room and by the time they let me in I have gone from sad and worried to really mad. I try to get it under control. It's so fucked up to go in and see someone who overdosed and almost died and want to kill them all over again. I don't want to kill him but I want to hammer him into the ground like a tent stake. Why can't he get his shit together like a normal person? I just don't fucking get it. What are your internal organs doing while that shit courses through your veins? Are they just struggling and weeping and crying trying to process this poison? Or am I full of shit because I drink alcohol and that's no more gentle on your interior. Peter lies in the hospital bed with an IV and bracelet. The back is tilted up and his skin is pale and all I can think is that we were young once we were young once we were young and didn't know that we would pollute ourselves and fall down these holes and sully everything that was good. Why did we waste all that time when we had clear skin and didn't pay rent?

I want to go back for just half an hour and really appreciate it. Appreciate our stupid outfits and cheap kickballs and tiny saws for cutting fallen branches. I want to go back and not hate him for a minute and hug him impulsively and know it's the most unfettered time we'll ever have together. I want to be a different kind of sibling, less intense, less angry. It might surprise you, but Peter was a very quick-to-forgive kid. He was emotional and volatile but he got over our tussles very quickly. One time he had a metal bow rake he was swinging around near where I was playing in our driveway, and he said he would hit me and I had to move. I was scared but knew I shouldn't give in to his tantrum. I stood at a safe distance and yelled for my mom and she didn't hear. I wish I could have talked him out of whatever upset him in that moment. I wish I had been nice. I wish I had done better. I don't remember what happened but it stopped eventually and I vowed to hate him for the rest of my life. I vowed I would never speak to him again. I knew I could make that happen. This is how sociopathic mafia dons are made. I don't know why I didn't end up killing people and running a crime syndicate, inspiring a great documentary. Instead I am soft and stupid and I can't do anything besides sell weed to celebrities. I can't think of a dumber "skill." Who would I have been if I hadn't taken the low road through everything? There's probably a life I didn't take, one in which I'm a marine biologist or work at the United States Treasury or something. Maybe I would be a tobacco lobbyist with no social conscience. We'll never know because I'm bearing down on this feral existence and it's too late to be anything but what I am, fingers in the dam, temporarily holding back ten leaks and watching new ones sneak through.

While I sit next to my brother's bed waiting for him to straighten out, I decide to write a stand-up set as a piece of shit.

Lights come up. The stage is empty, except for a pile of wadded-up toilet paper on a silver serving platter that is nearly consumed by a reeking pile of feces.

"Good evening, everyone! Man, I feel like shit."

People flip out! This line just came from an actual turd!!

"Have you guys ever noticed that most people stink? They walk into a room and you're like what just happened? Did the sewer just burp a brown dolphin into my lap? The kind tourists would pass around to take photos of until it died? And then you're like, oh, it's just a person. And they don't know how to act.

"Hey, I'll tell you the truth, I bottomed out one time. I dropped out of what I'd always considered my home, a tight tube of a place, and landed deep under water. Just when I was starting to acclimate to my new porcelain swimming pool, I was sucked down to an even lower level. This is not a euphemism for the Republican party! It's my life, save your metaphors. Or try another. One minute you think you're the byproduct of a sub-standard lunch, and that the effort to exist was your end game. The next minute it turns out you have a whole new journey to take as this reeking piece of shit. You really don't want to be one of the ones that requires you to jiggle the handle. You don't want to leave little guys behind. It's my version of being caught in the criminal justice system.

"I've tried to explain to people what it feels like to be me and I don't always get it across. People don't want to hear about what it feels like to be shit, or to touch shit. Reach out and touch me! Many people simply haven't cleaned up after their dog or large cat, and they've never changed a diaper (don't even get me started on a baby's warm projectile diarrhea). If they're not working in a zoo of any traditional kind, how could they know! Not everyone can be the hooker willing to pull out a Folgers can full of turds you've been saving for a month for a finger paint party on a tarp in the garage. For some that is foreplay, and who are we to judge?

"What's the best way to get a turd to come out and play?

"Metamucil!

"What's the first thing a turd says when it wakes up in the morning?

"Cannonball!

"How do you know when you've had enough roughage in any one day?

"There are stock photos of you laughing and a Tumblr making fun of it!

"Do you need to stop jogging as a hobby just because you've pooped behind rocks, next to parked Volvos and in your shorts innumerable times whilst trying to complete some modest laps around Bernal Hill? In the grand scheme of how all of humanity treats each other, takes care of the planet and reveres its wildlife, no! Not on my watch!

"Do girls in junior high have a special corner on the market of feeling like a piece of shit? Are magazines and society in general crucial to crafting this feeling? I would say with relative confidence that there are not enough wet wipes in the world to clean our country's hairy, recalcitrant anus.

"There is a difference between being a piece of shit and feeling like shit. A piece of shit rarely feels like what they are. The auto-erotic bronzing they've performed on themselves makes them impervious to clarity. I doubt I need to tell you those are rose-colored glasses perched on the schnoz of a shit-head. They're the portals to the brown sound, the rumbling low tone that generates an auditory vibration that reaches into your bathroom area and wiggles the poop out of your intestines. The brown sound. Available inaudibly at libraries and video stores, two institutions whose presence has diminished dramatically over the last ten years owing to the extraordinary popularity of the internet. The internet! What do you do there? Insult people you don't know and find yourself reflected in a novelty T-shirt you can buy! What is the best use of this internet? Fomenting and supporting political movements. What is the worst use? Causing injury of emotional and physical nature. What do we do about it? Stop using plastic bags, dummy."

Hours later Peter gathers his belongings and a nurse comes in.

"Couple things before you go," he says. "Has your abdomen or lower back been bugging you?"

"Sort of," Peter says, cranky.

"One of your tests shows heightened enzymes in your pancreas. Before you leave, make an appointment to come back and get an ERCP. Could be pancreatitis, which is serious. I recommend staying away from alcohol at the very least before you get tested, or you could be back here much sooner."

"Great," Pete responds and pushes past the nurse to leave.

"I'll be sure he does that," I say to the guy, and follow my brother out.

Peter passes the front desk without stopping. "Hey," I call to him. "You need to make that appointment."

"I'll do it later."

"Come on, do it now, while you're here," I plead. He

keeps walking. "Get the fuck back here and make that appointment. Don't put me through all this shit and then be an arrogant fuck to top it all off." I holler, using the most assertive and hostile voice I have. Peter turns on his heel and marches to the counter, where a nurse in rainbow-print scrubs sits.

"Your sister ain't taking your crap today!" the nurse says, friendly.

"She's a real bitch!" Peter says with fake cheeriness.

The nurse studies Peter's face, then says, "I see selfish guys like you come in here all the time. Breaking your family's hearts. You can come in next Wednesday at eleven for your test. Now get out of here."

I mouth "Thank you" at the nurse, and we leave. I drive Peter to his car, which is still at the motel. It feels horrible to return to this place.

Peter gets out of the car without a word. I turn my car off and get out too. He loads his stuff into the backseat of his Forerunner, and as he's getting in the front, I say, "Peter. What now?"

"I gotta go to the farm."

"Rigo is bummed on you."

"Don't talk about me to other people."

"He's sick of your dope habit and so am I. You need rehab or something like that."

"Can I get in my car now?"

"You can do whatever you want. That's the sad thing."

He gets in his car and leaves. I decide to drive the two hours to my parents' house.

I park my car and see lights on inside. I'm sure it's my mom who is awake; she loves being up late and listening to old records in the living room. She is surely blowing through some crappy celebrity gossip magazines and enjoying a Sam Cooke record. My dad is long asleep, no doubt. Lying on his back with his arms crossed on his chest like a dead person, with his old cat Nobbit softly sleeping on his legs.

I let myself in, and my mom sits up.

"Intruder alert!" she says with a smile. "I didn't know you were coming!"

"I texted you but you probably didn't see it."

"Is everything okay?"

I lean my head on my mom's shoulder and sigh heavily. She pats my head.

"I'll make tea, unless you need something stronger," she says, and walks officiously to the kitchen.

"Tea is fine."

On my drive down here, I decided I would rent a place in Los Angeles for a while. I've only been doing this work for a couple months, but I can't imagine something better will come along. Plus I'm really enjoying L.A. So much of it feels cartoonish, like Pier 39. The parts that are downtrodden are so absurdly, abjectly squalorous that they also feel like a heightened, if depressing, reality. I don't have to come up to Northern California to re-up on product, I can meet someone in Bakersfield or whatever. Rigo has offered it before. I've just wanted an excuse to come up and check on Peter. I think I need to give up on that.

My mom comes back in the room with tea and we sink into the weirdly large leather couch.

"Peter is having a hard time," I say.

"Oh no," she responds, and her face stiffens. She grips her mug.

"I was just with him and I know he's okay right now, but it seems like he's, well," I can't say everything I want to say. I can't find it. I can't find what's true and what's okay to say. I feel enraged at my brother for being such a fuck-up. "I think he's struggling with heroin again."

"Oh no. Goddamn it." my mom says. "What do we do?" she asks with a sincerity that hurts.

"I don't think we can do anything."

"Where is he now?"

"Ukiah."

"Should we drive up there?"

"What I'm saying is, I don't think we can do anything. And for what it's worth, I think he's clean at the moment. I don't know if he'll stay that way." I look at my mom and feel like I'm betraying her. Like I'm hurting her. I feel awful. Her face doesn't really change. She's weathered this up and down with Peter for so many years. She didn't get what she expected out of life. She didn't get the sweet and normal kids her friends got.

"Okay. I'll call him tomorrow. Do you think he needs money?"

"He definitely doesn't need money."

"Should I find him an acupuncturist?"

"Mom," I say, more harshly than I want to. "I'm sorry there are no action items, I just wanted you to know what's going on."

"Don't get mad at me, young lady. You have no idea what it's like to be a mother."

"I know. I'm sorry." We sit in silence. I stare at her and she looks away. We reach the end of side one of Joni Mitchell's *For the Roses*. I flip the record.

Through a few connections I find a place in Hollywood. It's just a room in someone else's house, a DJ named Floss. Is it supposed to sound like "Flaws"? What is the point? A boring poetry of confessed imperfection? He sleeps all day and I rarely see him. Pretty perfect. My walls are lined with tall shelves stuffed with Floss's records. It feels very cozy though they would probably all spill out and crush me if there were an earthquake. I wonder if I would hear my own bones crack before dying? Or what if I lived and was the first real-life Flat Stanley? There's no way I could be first, people get crushed under falling things all the time, particularly concrete buildings and pianos.

I don't want to get my own house until I know I want to stay down here. It feels amazing to make as much money as I do with so little overhead. I went out to the Nude Bowl to skate a couple weeks ago. It's a left-hand kidney-shaped pool that used to be part of a nudist colony in the seventies or something. I buried a couple cans of money out there. Not right next to the pool, out in the brush. I marked the locations on my phone. It's so empty around there, I'm willing to take the chance. Maybe one of these days I can be a person who makes a treasure map of all the money I've hidden around California. There can be an article about me in *Billionaire Lifestyles* or *National Geographic*. I could also find a way to get this dough invested and blow it up into giant wads of cash but that's not as fun as being an eccentric weirdo. Do eccentric weirdos know that that's what they are? Maybe in this day and age they do, when there are stores like Hot Topic and you can subscribe to a look rather than come to it out of necessity.

I'm going to a comedy open mic at Little Joy tonight. Echo Park. A slim willow of a man dressed all in black stands at the door checking IDs. I smile in a very huge and unnecessarily sincere way as though I were selling perfume at a booth in a mall. I order a tequila and soda then sign up on the open mic list. It's a Monday night. There are a lot of people here, which does nothing to calm my nerves. I smoked a little UK Cheese before going out to get right in my head. It's a rad strain of sativa that is particularly good for creativity and focus. I edge in on a tall table and pull out my phone to look at the notes I made for my set. I inhale my drink quickly and go to the bar for another. My heart is anxiously pounding. It would be bad to back down now though. I would feel too delicate and like such a loser.

I'm somewhat buzzed and I'm hoping that makes me looser for my time onstage. I worry I'm going to shut down and not be funny. At the finish of my second drink I wonder if I should have stopped at one. I try to dig deep into my body, like a drunk Russian gymnast or stoned Muay Thai fighter. I should be able to access my skills regardless of my mental state or other influencers! The body memory exists! The cellular truth shall not be denied, assuming you can find it.

A lady with long brown hair and heavy black glasses gets onstage and starts the show. She looks like someone who doesn't notice her body much. She probably doesn't even talk about it being hard for women in comedy because she knows no other way. She's a woman, but a bro, but a woman. Like Cameron Diaz. My friend went to high school with her (Cameron) and said she's really nice.

The people on the list are funnier than I thought they would be. My chest tightens and I feel like I can't get a good, deep breath. I go out to the bar for a quick shot of tequila then I buy myself a Coke to be normal. The host calls my name so I walk straight up to the microphone. I trip as I step onto the stage and catch myself, though my Coke sloshes onto the floor. I should have left it on my table. Adrenaline surges through me. I step to the mic and unlike in the movies, there is no high-pitched squeaking feedback.

"Hey, you guys, sorry to be so cool right off the bat," I say, referencing my stumble. "I'm just adhering to the rules of women in entertainment, taking a spill so you like me. Do any of you feel like the whole body thing is a total sham? Especially when you're female. Your sense of your self and your body is destroyed so early in life that there's no real reason to keep the thing around unless you're attached to shitting yourself from stress. If you're going to shit yourself, and I don't suggest that you do, I would recommend doing it at home while naked and sitting on the toilet or at least reclining on a garbage bag on the patio. Sadly I've never had the opportunity to choose when it happens and I have shat myself while running, looking at vintage furniture, while on a walk miles from my home, and probably other occasions I'm not thinking of." Is self-deprecating humor the spiritual equivalent of tripping and falling? Am I still being a subjugated lady by soiling myself with these stories of being a non-dominant woman? Who cares.

That's the bulk of what I memorized, and I think it went over pretty well. I heard some laughs, and I do believe a single guffaw. I have a couple minutes left so I decide to wing it.

"Men. I've fucked some." A couple titters. "If there's one thing men make me question, it's the gender binary. And my ability to be a satisfying date because I just want to drink beer and watch TV like them. Who's going to cook and do the laundry if neither of us wants to?" The room is fairly quiet. I pause and panic sets in. I'm being terrible again. I can't leave on a low note. I have to find my way back or I'll never do stand-up again, and I feel like I have to do stand-up again, just to give my life texture while I'm tumbling around this big dumb planet. Goddamn. "Does anyone else find this weird? This format of telling jokes onstage?"

"No." Someone says from the audience.

"Okay, me neither," I say. Small laugh from one person.

"Yeah, girl," another person yells.

"I just hope you all come to understand the gift that is the daytime soap opera because it is a women's art form and it is disappearing," I say and put the microphone back. I get offstage and there is some sparse clapping. I know I messed up again. This is way harder than I thought it would be. I'm going to find more open mics and work on my set and next time I won't drink as much beforehand. It seems less funny now to be a mediocre comic. I'm going to have to try to get better at it.

My mom calls to tell me Peter went to rehab again. She says this time he's going to some kind of cheap rehab because he had to pay for it himself. I haven't written to him in weeks. I feel burned out on the whole relationship.

One month later, Pete's out of rehab. He's been texting me and trying to call me. It sounds like he has a pressing need to talk to me, which probably means something like making amends. I feel a lot of dread at the idea of having a phone call on the topic of emotions. I tell him I'm busy for several days, until he pins me down about it.

"How long are you going to avoid this?" he asks.

"Can you blame me?"

"No."

"Can't we text about it?"

"If we could I already would have. Can I just call you?"

So I call him. "What?" I say flatly when he answers.

"Jesus," he says.

"I don't want to be on the phone."

"Well here it is: I'm sorry I've been so fucked up for so many years."

"Okay."

"I'm sorry I hurt you with my actions."

"Are you doing a twelve-step thing or something?"

"Yes."

"Cool. Well thank you."

"Do you forgive me?"

"Sure."

"Paloma! Can you take this seriously please?"

"I am! It's a fucking lot! I can't process years of shit in one second, especially when I didn't expect to."

"That's fair. Can I come down and visit you?"

"Don't you have to work on the farm?"

"Rigo doesn't want me there right now. Maybe in a month or two."

"I guess you can come. When?"

"I got nothing but time. You tell me."

"Whenever."

"Tomorrow?"

"Whoa." I try to think of any reason for him not to come but can't come up with anything. "Okay, tomorrow."

Peter texts me that he's an hour away. I'm in bed watching TV. I get totally absorbed in a documentary about Albert Fish. Old people can be so devious.

Peter arrives and he's hungry, so we walk to Zankou Chicken for dinner. I get extra garlic dip with my quarter dark chicken plate. It makes me burp and fart like a middle-aged dad, but I don't care. I love it. I don't understand why anyone orders white meat. One year I had Thanksgiving with Irma at her mom's house and her mom just got a turkey breast since it was only the three of us. I couldn't believe anyone would do that to themselves. But she read that white meat was healthier than dark and Irma's dad died of a heart attack. It was painfully bland. It almost makes me angry to even think of people serving white meat to an unsuspecting dinner guest.

Peter looks a little worn. Tired. His eyes look more sunken than I've seen them.

"You okay, duder?" I ask him.

"What does that mean?"

"Like do you feel stable? Does this round of sobriety feel any different than the last?"

"Why?"

"It didn't work last time, why would it work this time?"

"Jesus, dude! I'm going to do the best I can. Fuck. I need a cigarette."

"Let's go outside, you can smoke in the courtyard."

"I just drove a long way to see you."

"I'm sorry! It's a lot of up and down with you and it's stressful!"

"I got it. Loud and clear."

"What do you want to do tonight?"

"Can we just watch a movie or something at your house?"

We walk home in comfortable silence. We stop at a bodega for treats. My brother gets a bag of sour gummy worms. I get a Pabst tall boy. We go to my house and I put on *Enter the Dragon*, one of our favorites. Peter lies in the bed I made for him on the floor, and I get in my single bed. A single bed! It's just the way Floss had this room furnished. I guess he thought maybe a nine-year-old would rent the room.

The movie starts and I look down at Peter on the floor,

the movie flashing in his eyes and his mouth downturned. One of his arms holds a blanket to his chest. I see his arm hair, and the way his knuckles fold his fingers around the blanket. He was a child once. He is this simple creature, a tender soft human, a person who shares my DNA. He's such a weird mess, and under all the chaos he's created I see his soft face, like when we were little, worried and searching.

"Pete," I say. He looks at me. "Come here and let me hold you." He looks back at the screen. Then he gets up and lies on my bed. I put my arm around him and we watch the movie. For a second I grab my phone and take a picture of us so I can remember this. I lean my head on him and hold him. He lets out a deep sigh, and I feel his body relax.

"I love you, my brother," I say.

"I love you, wombat," he replies.

Peter is back in san Francisco. He hasn't worked in over a month and I guess he joined a fucking adult lacrosse league. Lacrosse! No one in our family has ever played that sport. We're more of a swimming and running family. Sports of the ancients. No equipment beyond the relative majesty of your body. I guess he started dating someone from one of his twelve-step meetings. It sounds like he's really in love, though I can't figure out how that's possible when they've only been dating for a few weeks. He says they're not supposed to date in the first year of sobriety. I don't personally see why not, especially if you're feeling like shit all the time. It's probably nice to have a highlight. Pete says he doesn't know if he wants to keep going to meetings anyway; he says he's fine. I tell him I think he should keep going. If it gives you an edge on staying sober, why not? Every time he tries to just have a beer or somehow be only kind-of sober, which I guess is not sober at all, he ends up falling into this same shitty hole all over again.

I'm going up to visit Peter and get a handoff from the farm. He agreed to meet me in Oakland so I don't have to go into San Francisco. It saves me a little time. A couple days ago, he texted me that he and the woman he was dating broke up. It was a very brief exchange:

"Nala broke up with me. Bummed."

"What happened?" I responded.

"I fucked it up. I suck."

"No, come on," I wrote, and I didn't hear back. He has always isolated himself hardcore when he's upset. We're supposed to meet at a coffee place near where I'm meeting Hayden, the woman from the farm. I'm just going to trust he'll be there since he's not writing me back.

I meet Hayden in the parking lot of a Safeway off the 580 freeway. She's a tall black girl, her hair is a natural afro about five inches long. Super pretty. She's wearing a long skirt over jeans and a bulky sweater. Not too many African-Americans work on weed farms. What's fucked up is that so many have been arrested for nonviolent marijuana-related offenses, so I have to wonder, how many black folks are benefiting from legalization?

"Hey Paloma," Hayden says and hands me a couple non-descript-looking reusable grocery bags heavy with weed. I slide them under the back seat of my car and take some more.

"How are things on the land?" I ask.

"Real good, we're trying some new stuff with light deprivation, you're going to have some dope new product next time we meet."

"Stoked. Okay, by any weird chance have you talked to my brother?"

"Nah, but Rigo probably has, right?"

"I'll check. Be good, see you next time." We kiss each other on the cheek and Hayden is off.

I drive the short distance to the front of the coffee place, just so I can keep an eye on my car. I don't see Peter's car anywhere, but who knows, maybe he borrowed one. I go inside, and there are several people working on laptops at little tables. Harry Connick Jr. croons from the speakers. Peter's not there, so I order a coffee from a teenager with big ear stretchers and play a game on my phone.

After an hour, I get worried. I text Rigo and he hasn't talked to Peter in over a week. I text Irma, because they've hung out in San Francisco a few times since he's been back. She hasn't seen him for a few days. I decide to meet up with her in San Francisco.

My phone rings while I'm on the Bay Bridge. It's early evening. I don't recognize the number, but because I'm stuck in traffic, I decide to answer to entertain myself.

"Hello?"

"Hi, um." A woman's voice, I didn't recognize her. "Are you a relative of Peter Aberg?"

"Why?"

"Do you know him?"

Immediately, I'm annoyed that whoever this is probably wants money. Like maybe because of something he did, or his rehab, I don't know. Maybe a collections call and he gave my number instead of his own, the idiot. "I'm not going to tell you if I know him, so just tell me what this is about."

"Well," she hesitates. "He's dead."

"What are you fucking talking about?"

"You don't have to believe me, but I'm telling you, he's dead. I work at the Travelodge on Valencia and Market in San

Francisco, and he was here last night, then he didn't check out this morning like he was supposed to and we kept knocking and he didn't come out so we had to call the cops. That's standard when someone doesn't check out and we can't get in the door because they put that bar lock on. There's no way to open a door with that lock on, isn't that crazy? The cops went in through a window and found him lying on his bed. Just alone and dead. I got the officer's badge number and the number at the station if you want it."

"How did you find me?"

"I took one look at him, he was a good-looking guy, he had a nice car, nice clothes, I knew he wasn't homeless or anything. I knew he had to have family around somewhere so I looked online and you were listed as P. Aberg in San Francisco. I'm really sorry."

"Well I don't mean to be rude, this is just a lot to try to understand. Give me the number for the police guy and I'll try to figure this out."

We hang up and it strikes me as so weird that the person who gave me the shittiest news of my life would always just be a voice to me, would move on with her day, talk to people, maybe tell them what happened at work, and then she'd get a Coke from the fridge and hear about someone else's day, stained for a minute or a day or a week by what she saw, but then moving on.

I call around until I locate the medical examiner's office, where my brother's body will be held overnight. I've gotten through the tunnel and I'm inching toward the Fifth Street exit.

"So is there any chance he's going to live, like he might wake up or something?" I ask the guy at the Medical Examiner's office. I want to be sure, so I know if I should go ahead and be sad or brace myself to be furious with him for getting me involved in more shit. Part of me wants him to be dead so I have something definite, not another narrow escape and sprawling uncertainty.

"If he's here, he's definitely dead," the guy, Gene, says. "Any chance you can come and identify the body?"

"Yeah." I wait a moment until I can identify my own body.

"We're at 850 Bryant. Open all night. But the sooner the better."

"Okay."

I decide to call my parents. My mom answers.

"Mom."

"Hi honey, what's going on? Are you outside?"

"Mom I have something really terrible to tell you. Really really terrible."

"Oh no."

"Peter is dead. He died last night. They said it looks like he OD'd."

"Oh no, that can't be, I just talked to him yesterday. Oh no. Oh no."

"Well it happened last night so I guess that's possible." I feel anger well up in my chest, like any gesture toward denial is an extension of what got us here. I feel full of rage but keep it in check while I remind myself that my mother, this beautiful human who didn't ask for this, is getting the worst blow of her life. It shatters me.

I tell her what little I know and she gets off the phone to talk to my dad.

I park on the street right outside the medical examiner's office. I check the meter to see if it's running. It is. I have coins. I know there's not a congruency to what moments you have to pay for in life, when you have to lay down some dough to get what you want or to confront unjust horrors. It feels like the height of absurdity to be captured at a parking meter inserting coins and watching the numbers go up. I have to estimate the time I will need to identify my brother's body at the medical examiner. How long will I need? Will I overshoot and drive away thinking well, the next person coming to identify the body of a loved one won't have to pay that damn meter! Or will I come out, see an expired meter and be glad I didn't get a ticket? Or come out and see a ticket, and fill with self-pity like a sad lady who fills her bathtub with water, bath beads and a silly child's plastic whale toy that she repeatedly pulls the string on and watches it putter around in her sad bath and it mirrors so perfectly the repetition, cuteness and futility of her malaise? I fill that meter to the max and walk inside.

The whole building is a heavy concrete monster, like walking into the side of a mountain. I pull open the stupid creaking glass door and face a counter. Three mismatched chairs straight from a grade school in the 1980s sit behind me, for waiting. Waiting! Like you would do for something you want! But also for a pap smear I guess. And a dead brother. The ceilings are very tall and fluorescent lights hang impassively over several desks, tweed padded dividers, filing cabinets and your average mound of paperwork. A man comes to the counter in a short-sleeved white shirt and glasses. He has grey hair and a mustache. A kind face. I tell him my name and he hands me a large manila envelope.

"I'm Gene. We spoke on the phone. Here's the stuff we found with your brother," he says. "There's a cell phone in here that's been ringing all night but whenever I answer it, the reception in here is so bad I can't understand what the guy is saying other than his name, Rigo or Diego or something. There've been a few other calls, I wrote all the numbers

137

down." I look inside the envelope and see the cell phone, some random pieces of paper with notes on them, a phone charger, his driver's license, all the stupid stuff you have with you when you die. The things you can't carry into the next life like your Lamborghini and your trophies. A lesson in what matters.

"Are you ready to go in and identify the body?" Gene asks.

"Well yeah, but my dad is on his way and he'll be here in an hour. Can I have him see the body too?"

"We don't normally do that. This isn't a viewing, it's just to get him identified."

"I understand," I say, though I do not want to understand, I want to fight, for no reason, in a purely contradictory and ideally abject manner. "But I know my dad, and it's just," I feel greedy asking for this, and for thinking my feelings carry any weight in a public institution. "He will never fully believe my brother is dead if he doesn't see his body here." I think of my dad and his disconnect from reality, his wild preference for delusion over truth. I know I can't live with the crushing sadness of him thinking Peter might be alive so I want him to see his son's body. Which is so despicable of me, in this way, to be the architect of this horrific moment. But I guess Peter has a hand in this too. So here we were, collaborating on exacting this awful fate on our parents.

Gene takes me down a hallway and through a door into a small room. There are three pieces of '70s furniture covered in a dark green vinyl which would capture a hefty price in the right vintage store. I wonder if anyone ever sits on them. I choose to stand, and look at a long rectangular window with slim white plastic blinds closed over it. Gene stands to the far right of the window with the cord to the blinds in his hand. He pauses a second, then gives it a harsh yank and the blinds fly up, revealing a brightly lit white room with a gurney in it, and Peter lying on top. I don't gasp, I don't emote at all. I swallow air and still myself. I stare. Peter's face is incomprehensibly still. My eyes search for movement, even invent movement where I think it should be. I worked at a Buddhist HIV/AIDS hospice in the Castro years ago, and every time someone would die, the same thing happened. I couldn't comprehend the lifelessness of the physical form. I always suspected they were in there somewhere, and might roar back to life like a lawnmower that just needed several yanks of the rip cord to get started.

Pete has a fucking goatee. Who let that happen? I wonder if he'll be cremated or buried. There is a purple splotch spilling over one side of his face.

"What is that on his face, the big bruise? I mean why is it there?" I ask Gene.

"I don't know," he says.

There is a white sheet pulled up to Peter's shoulders.

I walk outside and call Irma while I wait for my parents. I tell her Peter is dead. She immediately starts crying and offers to come down, but I ask her not to. I don't want to figure out what to say to her as we weirdly hang out at the medical examiner's office. I would say things just to say things and I know I would feel fully embarrassed of my numb mezzanine-level mental state. It's an hour and a half from my parents' house so there's another hour before they arrive. I walk out to the sidewalk and look down at all the bail bond signs glowing on Bryant Street. The sky is navy blue but not particularly dark with all the street lights. I don't want to walk around. I'm worried the doors to the medical examiner will be locked for some weird reason or my brother will be lost, or my parents won't know how to get inside. I go back into the office and sit in one of the hard plastic chairs. I stare at the lights and try to absorb their atmosphere in a cinematic way. Like if I ever make a film of this moment, I have to remember exactly how it feels. For that reason I must note the dull buzz of the lights.

My parents finally arrive and by the grace of Gene we look at Peter's body together. My dad starts sobbing and then my mom does too.

What do you get when you have a living sister and dead brother?

Salt and fish bones, a washer with a blow dryer, a bicycle and a tar pit.

How do you know you're branded for life?

Everything you write is about dead family members.

How many decisions by young parents determine how their kids will turn out?

Not very many.

I follow my parents back up to their house in Calistoga. Every moment on the freeway feels surreal. Like I am driving a new reality with me but I haven't eaten it yet. I think about random shit. Stupid things I've said, people I've hurt, people who have hurt me, and I think about Peter and his face. I think about us talking. I think about how much we look alike. I think about us watching *Enter the Dragon* together in Los Angeles and not knowing that was it for us. I want to distract myself, and also I don't ever want to talk to anyone again. We are a middle-class family. An overdose is an aberration against upward mobility, a crime against decorum. No matter how many people in your family die of alcohol-related conditions, a drug overdose will always be a splatter of ugliness across your family portrait.

When we get to my parents' house, my dad mixes us all drinks. Gin and soda with lime. I sit on the floor in our living room and dump out the manila envelope holding my brother's stuff. My parents sit behind me and my dad turns on the TV to a news channel. After about thirty seconds my mom clicks it off. I look and they are staring into their drinks. My mom puts her hand over my father's. Tears run down her face. I put my hand on her shin and squeeze.

I find an unfamiliar cell phone in the envelope. Peter's passwords all spell F-U-C-K so it's not hard to get into the phone. There are only seven numbers in his contacts, I suspect because this is a new phone or a second phone, something like that.

I call each of the numbers in Peter's phone. The first few, no one picks up. One of the numbers is for a guy who answers his phone in English and when I ask him if he knew my brother he switches to Spanish. My Spanish is pretty good but he just keeps saying he doesn't know and can't understand me and then he hangs up on me.

The last number I call is for a guy named Tom. An answering machine picks up, it crackles and stutters with an old tape playing the outgoing message. The guy speaking, Tom, sounds crazy tweaked on speed. I imagine he is the guy who sold Peter the shit he bought and died from because the time and date of the calls in Peter's cell phone are just a few hours before they think he died. The machine beeps and I hang up, then dial the number again. No one answers, just the machine. I call and hang up about twenty times. I imagine calling this number over and over again, and terrorizing this person for the rest of my life. I bet I could do it. I could call every day a few times, leave creepy messages telling the dude he has blood on his hands. But maybe he doesn't. Maybe Peter orchestrated his own death, pure and simple. Maybe getting obsessed with some piece of shit drug dealer, another guy who is someone's son and brother and the source of significant pain for them, is pursuing a route through life that is ultimately without reward and will never mask the absence of my brother. It's so creepy to think about Peter dealing with this guy. I decide not to tell my parents anything about what the phone calls reveal, or don't reveal, because there is no value in these calls. Only heartache.

We ping around in the house for days, focusing on tasks. I do sleep at night. That seems wrong. Why can I sleep? One night I dream I'm standing on a bucolic hillside, watching a red-nosed pit bull run around at top speed, happy and exhilarated. Out of the corner of my left eye I see my brother standing next to me. I know he's trying to be near me, but not scare me. He smiles. We are content.

We have to pick out a casket. We find a funeral home online, one with lots of good reviews. People took the time to review funeral homes! What a time to be alive and burying someone dead! We go to Ballhorn's Funeral Chapel in downtown Santa Rosa. A gentleman named Fred greets us with a comically calm and quiet voice when we enter, and tells us that if we need anything, to let him know. He is a short white man, wearing a beige suit with a yellow shirt, and a perfect part in his blonde hair. The wall in the showroom (*showroom!*) is lined with a display of mini caskets. Little versions of big things are such perfect comedy. I imagine large dolls being placed in each, and having a theatrical funeral for many dolls at once. I would enlist a child to be a priest at their ceremony. I would film it like Todd Haynes filmed the Karen Carpenter story with Barbies. The idea of children born into moroseness is wonderful to me. I don't want anything bad to make them that way, just an innate grim sensibility and passion for funerals (and no injury to living things).

After looking around for a bit, my mom, dad and I sit down with Fred at a long wood table. I feel like we're in a play. I notice Fred has a little cross tattooed on his thumb, and I glimpse a similarly homemade tattoo peeking out his collar.

"Okay," he says in his quiet voice, with a strong Midwestern (maybe Wisconsin?) accent. "So one plot is five hundred dollars. Two plots are a thousand dollars. You can see the savings with the purchase of more than one plot." He gives us a closed-lip smile.

Abruptly my mom, dad and I are smiling and looking at our hands, trying not to dissolve in giggles. It would be the kind of laughing that if we let it happen, it won't stop until we throw up or injure ourselves. Thank the Gay Goddess for this sweet dummy at the funeral home. He is shining some light into our day.

I'm bummed we aren't going to cremate my brother's body or do an ecological burial that turns his body into a patch of mushrooms. (Whoa, wouldn't it be *nuts* to eat a bunch of dead person mushrooms? Would you dream about their childhood or something?) It is such a silly ritual to put a dead body in an ornate box. Why do we want to pack up this meaningless vessel? At least we choose a cheap casket. Not pine box cheap, but one step up. The veneer is a sparkly, shiny baby blue. Very downscale Liberace, or 1980s prom wear. Goodbye, blue sky.

The funeral is set for a couple of days later. First we have to mail a copy of Peter's death certificate to his fucking cell phone company so he can get out of his contract. Can you believe that? Do they have a fucking stack of death certificates that go into their big dumb shredder at a certain point? Once a week? Ongoing, mixed with old invoices? That would be so foul to be the person who takes the death certificates, finds the accounts and deletes them, then recycles the paper. There is such an ugly cloud of inhumanity around cell phone companies, cable TV companies, and any kind of insurance.

We have to find clothes for Peter to be buried in. My parents and I go to Target and picked out a pair of pants, oxfords, and a pack of tube socks. My dad and I split the remaining pairs in the pack. We got something so much worse than the brown acid by going to this brightly lit store to buy clothes for my brother to be buried in.

The day of the funeral arrives. I look through my clothes. Nothing appropriate. I pick out black jeans and a somewhat sweatshirt-y thing that is dark grey. I don't know what else to do. I don't wear dresses. It's fine to be myself today, right? What about other days? When I go out to the front hall my mom is there, dressed in a sapphire blue corduroy jumpsuit. With gold ballet flats. I truly didn't see this kicky, playful outfit coming.

"You look nice, mom," I say.

"You do too, honey."

"You don't think it's bad that I'm so casual?" I ask.

"Oh, who cares. Doesn't matter."

"Where's dad?"

"Backing the car out. Let's go."

We drive over to the church in silence. I want to make casual conversation, try to be light and funny. But then I realize I don't have to. We can just be this way, internal and sad.

We park at Ascension Lutheran, where my brother and I were baptized. A simple wood exterior, a tall, pointy roof at one end. We go inside, where a few of my parents' friends have already gathered. It will be a closed-casket ceremony. The bruise-like mark on Peter's face upset my mom, and she prefers we keep that private. I want to argue against this, like it's my job to make everyone face facts. But I realize how pompous that is, and that I can just put aside the idea of trying to adjust how other people think into my way of doing things.

More people arrive, and I spend time chatting with my parents' friends. I see them searching my face for sadness or angst. I smile like a real estate agent, huge and never-ending. I like seeing all the old family friends. I don't like the idea of performing my grief for anyone. That will come on my own time, when I'm ready.

The ceremony is about to start, so I go and sit on a pew with my mother. My dad helps carry the casket in with a panoply of uncles. The pastor stands at the front. A guy plays a Grateful Dead song on guitar, I don't know the song. My mom hired him because my brother hated church and church music. Funerals are for the living, but my mom's gesture to his tastes is hiring this guitar guy. It's pretty sweet of her. I try to listen to the service but I'm impatient and just want to get the hell out. It's painful to wait and resist my urges to grunt and snort at the ritual of it all. Finally the casket is carried out to a hearse and we drive in a cumbersome, long line to the boneyard. We get out of the car and await the clumsy procedure of gathering around the casket on its casket-lowering apparatus. There is a skirt of Astroturf around the perimeter of the earth hole where this dumb body will live. There's talking, there's the hard pounding of my heart. We're all just bodies in space, until we're not.

It's weird cozying up to the mind fuck of losing a sibling. I drive down to San Francisco to see Irma on my way back to Los Angeles. We meet at a bar on 24th Street, Pop's. We sit at the bar and while we chat, a woman I know walks up to say hello.

She says, "I'm sorry to hear your brother died."

"Thanks," I say. I'm not interested in pursuing the conversation.

"You're really fucked. This will never leave you," she says. It's harsh, but I feel a sense of validation too. Irma tenses next to me. I feel pissed that she feels entitled to say this, to be the one who delivers that message.

I wait to feel tears in my eyes but nothing comes. "I think you're right," I say, and turn away.

I stay over at Irma's that night, peacefully and passively spooning with her on her sandy futon. She has two new kittens, Thelma and Louise, who jump around and pounce on my feet whenever I move them. It's incredibly soothing.

I drive back to my room in Los Angeles the next day.

I wish there was a dark comedy open mic I could go to. Where I could joke about my mom's blue funeral jumper and whatever else I would usually shy away from in fear of cringing, dismayed faces while I make fun of my life's darkest and saddest moments. I like comedy. I'm an animal. I'm a simple booger in the nose of life. I'm waiting to be picked, to get blown out of here, to fall. I'm a single-cell dipshit floating around in antifreeze in a campground parking lot. A stray mutt drinks from me. I'm a dirt clod on the sidewalk fallen from a ripped-up lawn. A small green worm eating geranium leaves. I'm a rusty staple in an ugly shoe. I'm trying to be the person I am meant to be, just a little ahead of schedule.

A lot of people to thank, a few to forget and feel terrible about forever. Thank you to my mom and dad. I'm not what you expected, but I'm mostly a pleasure, right? Enormous thanks to Michelle Tea who has believed in me and pushed me to flourish since 1995. I love you beyond. So much of what I've done as a writer has been at your urging. Eternal gratitude of the hormonal mind to Beth Lisick, my comedy partner and best friend, a beacon of love and joy in this world. So much gratitude to everyone who read my manuscript and gave me feedback. Thank you Maggie Nelson for such thorough, brilliant input. Thank you Elaine Katzenberger for your faith and commitment to making this a respectable book. Thank you Susan Spinks for encouraging me to write all the time!! Thank you Anina Bacon for encouraging me from the word go. Thank you Beth Stephens, Annie Sprinkle, and Rick Stine. Thank you skateboarding for the being the most fun, beautiful, fulfilling pursuit a person can have in this earthly body. Thank you Bob Lake for your endless encouragement in that realm (and all others). Thank you to all of my gorgeous friends for the love and support. Thank you Miriam Stahl for being such a rad business partner in Pave the Way, and making beautiful images to share with the world. Most of all, thank you to my passion partner, romantic colleague, love of my life Kristina Davies for loving me so perfectly and letting me love you. I'm a lucky, and very sexy motherfucker.